corona man

Also by D.M.Thomas:

novels
The Flute-Player
Birthstone
The White Hotel
Russian Nights Quintet:
  Ararat
  Swallow
  Sphinx
  Summit
  Lying Together
Flying in to Love
Pictures at an Exhibition
Eating Pavlova
Lady with a Laptop
Charlotte
Hunters in the Snow

verse novel
Vintage Ghosts

verse memoir
A Child of Love and War

poetry
Penguin Modern Poets 11
Two Voices
Logan Stone
Love and Other Deaths
The Honeymoon Voyage
Dreaming in Bronze
The Puberty Tree: *Selected Poems*
Dear Shadows
Not Saying Everything
Unknown Shores: *Collected SF poems*
Shadow Sonnets
Flight and Smoke
Two Countries
Mrs English and Other Women
Family Bible
The Last Waltz

translations
Akhmatova: *Selected Poems*
Pushkin: *Selected Poems*
          Onegin
          Ruslan and Ludmila
Yevtushenko: *A Dove in Santiago*

memoirs
Memories & Hallucinations
Bleak Hotel

biography
Alexander Solzhenitsyn: *a Century in his Life*
Coffee with Freud

stageplay
Hell Fire Corner

children's fiction
The Devil and the Floral Dance

See also dmthomasonline.net

corona man

a fictional verse journal
in the plague year

d.m. thomas

The Cornovia Press

SHEFFIELD

Published by The Cornovia Press, Sheffield, 2020

© D. M. Thomas 2020

ISBN 978 1 908878 18 2

For my friend Juliet Johns

1   *Voices*

I've got so used to being on my own,

No one to talk to but myself,

No other voice—of course my Elsie talks,

I don't count her, the dear of her,

I never listened to her when she lived,

She rattled on so, and does still,

Although she comes less as the years pass.

The lady at the post office when I went

To pick up my pension, she was kind,

She'd chat with me, but then they closed that.

I'd buy a paper there, but that's no loss.

The carers who came to get me up and dressed

After my illness, they were too rushed

To have me done and go, and nearly always

A different girl or chap. They did their best,

Asking me how I was, and so on,

But irritating, addressing me as 'young man',

Or straightaway 'John' when they didn't know me,

Not 'Mr Trenear'. It wasn't really talk.

The radio used to be a comfort, but the talkers

Mumble these days, in the end I gave up.

So there's been no one. Perhaps a 'Take care,'

From a checkout server at the supermarket.

Just my own voice, and I've grown bored with that.

So this has come as something of a shock.

It started with a phone call from my son

In Birmingham. He only phones at Christmas.

Not always then. Last year he forgot.

Well, I know he's busy, has his own family,

Kate and their two, Josh and Anita.

He called to ask me was I alright.

It stunned me, I had to sit down, shaky-like after.

Then there were people knocking at my window,

Waking me from my armchair drowse.

I thought they were the ghosts of my two aunts,

Who shared their lives, after wartime bereavements,

Two smiling faces, said they were volunteers

Come to see if I needed shopping done.

Hard to hear through glass but

They wouldn't come in, I don't know why that was,

I keep my little flat clean. But they seemed nice,

Shouting and smiling through the window.

They came back later with some bread and milk,

Leaving the bag outside. Another chat!

And then a chemist phoned, about my meds.

Four voices in one day! They're in my head now,

Thunderous, overwhelming...

                              The two good women

Said they would call again next week, and bring

Corona. I think that's what they said. My mind

Moved seventy years back, to when a lorry

Would stop outside our house, selling the drinks.

I thought that business shut down years ago.

I loved the cherryade, and the way it popped and fizzed

When you hooked the wires off from the top.

That was a good day, when the Corona man called,

And mother let me take the empty bottles

Back, and buy sweets with the money for them.

I've asked for cherryade. Of course it won't

Taste quite the same, for nothing ever does,

But I appreciate the human voices,

And it's some news, the next time Elsie comes.

2   *Mysteries*

I almost don't want to wake up no more,
Dreading the empty day, but still I do,
The darn heart keeps on ticking.
I lie there for a while, trying to dredge
Some memories of my dreams of voices, people,
Seeking a bit of real life. Mostly though
They've slipped away, like the people themselves did.

Then I hear Elsie say, You must get up,
Come on, don't let me down. And so I wash,
Shave, dress, and if the weather's fine,
Like it was today, I put on a nice shirt
And tie, for she always liked me to look smart.
I manage a short walk most days,
Using my frame. The streets are very quiet,
I don't know why that is.
I head for the garden seat outside
What used to be the library. Closed now.
Well, as I was sitting there today,
Catching my breath, I saw the lady who
Is like my Auntie Peggy, bless her heart,
Who've promised me Corona. I stood up,
Smiling at her, and went to shake her hand.

She leapt away from me, with a gasp
She changed into a smile, her face flushed,
And rushed away...

And what it did
Was to bring back a moment I thought I'd buried
From a few months before. At the supermarket,
I saw a little girl, aged about six, who looked
Like Jenny, with her short blond hair,
Waiting for her mother, going through checkout.
I wanted to give her a Kit Kat I'd bought;
I caught hold of her hand, she was smiling up at me
When her mum, with a face full of thunder,
Rushed up and grabbed her away.

It left me shattered, Elsie,
This time again. Was I so unpleasant? Smelly?
I'd put clean trousers on, and just in case,
Dabbed on some of that aftershave you gave me
The Christmas after our dear Jenny was born,
'Old Spice'. There's still a lot left
'Cause as you know I let myself get scruffy
For ages after she passed, poor little girl;
I couldn't laugh any more at comedy shows

I used to love, like 'Hancock's Half Hour',
'Take It From Here' and 'Around the Horne',
The heart gone out of me—of us, and 'Old Spice'
Pushed to the back of the cabinet.
I don't know why I put some on today.
But anyway, what I'm saying is, I don't smell,
Or at least didn't, when I took my walk.
Why did the lady back off? She seemed so nice.
Know, do you, Elsie?... It's a mystery
Like everything. I thought I knew, at twenty,
What life was all about, but now I'm old
It just gets more and more a mystery.
'Old Spice'... Where did they find those names?

My groceries came; I only briefly saw

My Auntie Peggy waving through the window.

I know she isn't Auntie but her greying curls

Are so like hers were. Some of my distress

At how she'd run from me was eased

By seeing she had had an accident,

Perhaps a fall, for she was bandaged up

Over her mouth and nose. Alas there was

No bottle of Corona in the bag.

She'd left, wedged between tins of Spam,

A message for me, her writing copperplate.

I read it in the lovely April evening

('All in an April evening', that gentle

Music comes back to me from hearing mum

And dad singing it in the chapel choir

Back home in Cornwall.) The message said,

'I must apologise for yesterday.

You caught me on the hop. I should have stopped

And spoken. Fear makes us rude. Forgive me.

I know the people hereabouts

Keep mostly in their own community

And many don't speak English well, but they

Admire you as an English gentleman,

Living alone but always so well dressed.
The oldest can remember how you cared for
Your wife, lingering with cancer, while not
Knowing anyone, unused to London. How
That must have felt I can't begin to imagine,
Both for you and your wife. You're very brave.'
She ended it 'Stay safe, Virginia Rudd.'

I read and re-read it, in my armchair.
What did she mean by fear? But more important,
She thinks I'm brave! and says the people here
Admire me! I was touched by that,
It's hard to know what people think, the women
Especially, their faces mostly veiled.
After a while I thought I'd go outside
Onto my tiny balcony, to see if I
Could catch the sunset between the high-rises.
I felt quite happy, thinking of her words.

Almost as soon as I was out and leaning
Above the giddy abyss, the west crimson
Where I could glimpse it, people appeared
On balconies in the two tower blocks

Visible from ours, and they started clapping!

And many were banging saucepans and pots.

Others, below, above me, were joining in.

My God they were saluting me! Virginia

Was right, they do admire me! She must

Have told them I crave contact. I had tears

Springing at once. I clapped my thanks,

Bowed, waved. Indoors, I slumped down, shaken

And deeply moved. My eyes went round

To the framed photos of my wife, of dear

Little Jenny, my mum and dad, and so on.

All gone. I thought, well, I deserve

The clapping and the banging. I am brave,

Dragging myself out of bed each morning

When almost all I've loved have gone

Into the other light.

But still, how kind of them it was, how kind.

4   *A musical dream*

For once, when waking, sunlight breaking through
My window, I still have a dream in sight.
There is an orchestra where the conductor
Decides this music doesn't need the horn,
Thinks it's too brash; oboe and clarinet
Make a more pleasing sound. I'm angry with him
And shout, 'I like the horn!
It's a great instrument, vibrant and strong,
I've always liked to have the horn,
And though I've less breath now and clumsy fingers
I can still play. We have to have the horn!'
Smiling, he says, 'You should age gracefully.'
'Go fuck yourself!' I snarl—and so I wake.

I rest, excited by my dream. Some life!
And I was younger in it—passionate.
I'm ashamed too, it's not like me to swear.
The only times I ever used that word
Were untold years ago, when Elsie and I
Were in love still, and making love,
And both used words that broke through the taboos,
Exciting ourselves more. Never since then.
And why, in God's name, dream about the horn?

I've never played it, and prefer the cello,

Assuming it is played by... that young girl

Who had MS. So tragic, with those gifts,

And such a beauty, her hair sparkling, tossing,

Her skirt spread wide, her entire soul bent

Over and into her lovely instrument.

I must find that old LP and play it.

I don't know what the dream meant. Nothing I guess.

An invitation to tea

The Elgar, Du Pré playing, left me tearful,
Despite the crackly sound, the stylus
Worn out. I couldn't find a new one
As CDs had come in. I hated that,
The loss of those great pictures on the sleeves
Of the LPs, which added richness to
The music: this one shows the sweep
Of lush green meadows and the Malvern hills
Where Elgar lived. The CDs' cellophane
Was like Fort Knox, and when you broke through that
The flimsy boxes often fell apart.
Besides, the sound is much less bright.
I like the crispness and warmth of an LP's tone.
The world's moved on from me.

I thought of Jackie, of that first wrong note
She played in—where was it? Carnegie Hall?—
In New York anyway. Poor girl, poor girl.
And if, in later years, as the disease
Crept over her, she took her sister's husband
To bed, with her agreement, as that film
Suggested, who is anyone to judge?
Not me, not me. The stylus might be damaged

Irreparably but she was still
No smooth, lifeless CD.

                              Afterwards, sad
And at a loss, I thought I'd write Virginia
A note for her to find when she collects
The empty bag outside my door...
'Dear Mrs Rudd, or may I say Virginia?
I was so grateful to receive your letter,'
And then went on to say how she reminded
Me of my Auntie Peggy: 'You've the same
Beautiful hair and smile and graceful movement.
Your figure too, if I may be so bold—
Peggy was also buxom. I like a woman
Who's not afraid of being womanly.
She never married, yet was always cheerful,
Hiding her grief for a love lost in war.
As a boy I had a crush on Auntie Peggy,
Once saw her, through a door
She'd left ajar, in corselette and stockings
And that was thrilling, as you may imagine!
It would be nice, Virginia, if one day
We could have tea together? Please excuse
My running on about my aunt. I really

Just wished to thank you. Sincerely, John Trenear.'

Well it was done. I slumped back in my chair,
Exhausted, thinking about my dream again,
The horn... So strange... 'We have to have the horn...'
Who was that great horn player?... Barry Tuckwell!
It's strange how often unimportant names
Come back, and yet I had forgotten Jackie's
Until I saw it on the record's sleeve.
I wonder if I have an ear infection—
Can't hear the rush hour traffic.

6   *Angel*

Elsie is nagging: 'Old fool, she won't come back.'

(The bag had gone when I woke up this morning.)

'Not after what you wrote. What is she—sixty

At most? An attractive mature woman;

And for God's sake you don't call a woman buxom

And think that she'll be pleased...'

But then the doorbell rang, and I jumped up,

Or to be truthful heaved myself from the chair,

Heart in my mouth, certain it was her.

But when I'd hobbled to the door and looked out

Through its glass panel I near fainted, it

Was not Virginia but the Angel of Death:

An immense female figure all in black

From head to foot. But then I saw a second

Figure, a man, beside her, darkskinned, bearded,

But smiling in a friendly way. Ah, Muslims!

The woman in a burka. Frightening,

I always keep well clear of them when out.

I opened the door; he said, 'I saw you waving

To the crowd on Thursday evening and I thought

It meant you needed help. My wife

Has cooked you something.' 'Please come in.'

She handed me a plastic bag... containers.

'We're not a threat,' the man said, entering;

'Allah protects us.' I don't know why they should

Have been a threat, they didn't look

Like terrorists. 'It's curry. My mother's

Recipe, and Fatima cooks it well;'—

Glancing aside at her and facelessly

She inclined her head. '—you like?' 'Thank you, I like.'

'Just heat it up.' I gestured to the sofa.

'No need to keep two metres, eh?' he smiled.

I didn't know what he meant, but muttered 'No.'

These were bad times he said, and I agreed;

The times are always bad. He asked if there

Were other things I needed, and I said,

'Well, I was promised Corona; I don't suppose...?'

He didn't understand—hardly surprising!

They didn't stay long. He firmly shook my hand

On leaving, and I looked to shake hers too,

But she seemed handless just as she was faceless

And the man shook his head. She glided out

Behind him.

        Her towering image stayed,

Like Lot's wife only black, and gradually

I learned to pity her. She speaks no English

Her husband—Aziz—told me, doesn't need it.
Our English life, outside their own four walls,
Is blank to her, the people hurrying past
Out in the streets, all with their own troubles
And problems—she knows nothing of them,
Of us. She must feel sad.

                              I dislike curry,
It wasn't a dish we knew when I was young,
And it's too hot for me. But I remembered
From Matthew 25 'I was anhungered
And ye gave me meat'. I was not anhungered
Literally, but they had fed me
In a deeper way. And so that evening
I warmed their gift up, and was thankful
For the rice and the strange aromatic bread.

7 *What wife?*

A letter on my mat, Virginia's elegant
Handwriting on the envelope. I had
To sit down, weak at the knees, before
I tore it open. 'Dear John,' I read, 'Thank you
So much for writing. It would be very nice
To have a cup of tea with you sometime
When this is over. For now, however, we all
Must keep our distance, and in fact I'm needed
For other caring duties. Emma, my wife,
The lady who was with me the first time,
Will bring your groceries in future.
Stay well and safe, yours faithfully, Virginia.'
I read it twice, three times, like an old boxer
Punchdrunk and so savagely battered that
He leans against the ropes, inviting blows
Into his stomach.
                    When I could think more clearly
I stared at just three words: 'Emma, my wife.'
It made no sense. Women don't have wives!
Had she missed out a word? 'My gardener's wife?'
'My butcher's wife?' I found myself crazily
Shouting a line from Shakespeare I had learned
For the Croydon Players fifty years ago,

'My wife! My wife! What wife? I have no wife!'
Yes, she must have missed out a word. But still,
She wasn't interested in me. Old fool,
As Elsie said. Too old for her. And yet
My heart has never felt younger; it's the world
That has grown old and stale. She couldn't see it.
Well, fuck her! I shouted it out. Everyone swears
These days. I'll join them. Emma, my wife.
What wife? She has no wife.

                  I took myself out.
In the piss-stinking lift, a white-overalled woman
Smiled, but pressed herself back, away from me,
Leaving me, returning her smile, feeling foolish.
The streets amazingly quiet. Just as I turned
A corner from our block a police car slowed,
Then stopped, and a young copper leapt out.
I shouldn't be out, he said; I asked him why.
'You know why,' and he seized my arm.
'Come along now; there's a good gentleman...'
Before I knew it I was in my flat,
Seething and mystified. Clearly there's something
Sinister happening in which the old,
Or perhaps only old men, aren't allowed out.

Zulu! Why was I being reminded of

That film? Ah yes, doesn't the RSM

Say something like that to the missionary,

Drunk, at Rorke's Drift? 'Come along now,

There's a good gentleman.' But that was kindly.

Not so this London. Something deadlier than Zulus

Is outside, watchful. 'We all must keep our distance.'

So distant and so careless of my feelings

She missed a word out—yet she talks of caring!

I know a better word for her starting with c

And should have known she wasn't trustworthy

When she didn't bring me the Corona.

You shouldn't make a promise you can't keep.

8 *In the gloaming*

I toss and turn all night, Elsie's last nightie
Still folded on the pillow to my left
As though awaiting her return. I've got
Zulu in my head, I don't know why, and just
Can't find the name of the actor playing
The missionary who with his buttoned-up
Daughter is watching a Zulu wedding dance.
She's agitated as barebreasted, dusky
Brides tease the young, nearly nude warriors,
Their spears outthrust and urgent.
Her father says to her, if I recall, '*What went*
Ye out into the wilderness to see?
A man dressed in soft raiment?' His name is Hawk,
Something like that... it's maddening,
I know it well... At last it comes to me—
Hawking, yes Stephen Hawking. A fine actor,
Also great in the film *The Crucial Sea*.
Later his cells went haywire, cancer I think,
He had a voice box fitted, so he croaked,
And then was in a wheelchair, paralysed,
His burly body shrivelled, twisted sideways,
And speaking like a Dalek. Turned to physics.
Fine as an actor and a physicist.

I must have watched *Zulu* a dozen times
And Tony, my son, and I would quote it at
Each other. He's never rung since that surprise
Call, and I always get his answering machine.
Well, fuck him.

                    'Come along now,
There's a good gentleman...' Cocky young cop;
But it brings back an earlier scene, that first
Night Plymouth was blitzed, when mum and I
Had come up from Penzance to spend a week
With Uncle Harry. There was this flash
And when I came around amid the ruins
I saw—well I was five, I just remember
An ARP warden picked me up in his arms
And said, 'Come with me sonny and don't look.'

I thought I'd try my ancient TV set
To see if it still worked. I gave up on it
Soon after Elsie passed; they talked in mumbles,
Not the Queen's English, and when you caught
A word or two it was mostly crude and cruel,
Even in so-called comedy programmes. But
I must find out what is happening to us.

It works; well, sort of, flickering up and down.
The pictures are frightening: men or women,
They could be either, in spacesuits working on
Bodies with wires from every orifice,
Lights flashing and the background icy, sterile.
Have we been taken over by aliens? I
Quickly switched off, could be contaminated
Even by watching. I don't trust anyone.
It's very possible Virginia is
One of the aliens, they're clever enough,
And may come from a planet where
Men have been done away with and so females
Marry each other, procreate by gloaming.
Is that the word? It's something like that anyway.
That could explain a lot. Must stay hawk-eyed.
It can't be gloaming quite; that means sunset.
'In the gloaming, O my darling,
Think not bitterly of me'... Mum and dad sang
That duet at concerts. I can hear them now.

Seeking the dot

Something was different. I didn't know what it was

At first, but then I realised that while

The streets below held that strange quietness

This morning the sky above was noisier.

Noise, but what noise? Ah yes, a constant thrum

Of helicopters, far more than usual,

As though a hundred accidents had happened

At once, and people needed ferrying

To hospital. Eating my breakfast toast

I pondered. Flashes of memory:

The drone of planes, all heading for Normandy,

We'd heard for hours before the news came through

Of the D-Day landings; a joyful day

For most, but for my Auntie Gwen the start

Of lifelong sadness. Then, though only seen

On a television screen in my parents' cottage

In Penzance, the attack on—what were they called?—

The Dark Towers in New York. Elsie and I,

And other members of our family,

Watched it appalled, while upstairs something far

More important to me was happening,

My mother dying. I went up to her

And she was agitated. 'Is there something wrong, dear?

You're looking... shook up.' 'Just a bad accident
In America, mum, nothing to worry about.'
'Pray for me, John,' she said, grasping my hand,
'I've many sins.' So I knelt down, and prayed.
She lingered for another week or so,
So why, I wondered, had that Dark Towers tragedy
Flashed into my mind, just now? I only had
To hear the whirling blades high overhead
And the unnatural silence far below,
As if everyone had fled in terror,
To find a reason. And what had my Muslim neighbour
Said to me when he entered? 'I'm no threat'
Or 'We're no threat', with an odd stress
On the first word. It seemed to me he knew
That others would be. I became icily cold.
London was such an obvious target
With its high-rises—like my own. Panicking,
I rushed out to the balcony and stared
Between and above the other high-rises
And spent the next hour or more straining
My eyes, seeking the first ominous black dot
In the empty blueness. Even if the great plane
Struck above me, the lift would be closed

And there'd be no way I could hobble down
The fourteen flights of stairs. So would I jump
Before the smoke and fire engulfed me?

I gave myself a sick headache, had to lie down.
Somehow I slept; and when I woke I felt
Much calmer, and could reason with my fear:
The people here were poor, why strike at us
And not Canary Wharf? And why kill Muslims,
So many of them here, if you were from
Bin Adam's tribe? In any case
What could one do?
                          I read a chapter
Of *David Copperfield*, and the familiar words,
From a book my parents gave me at thirteen
For Christmas, comforted as they always do.

10   *An offer from the Council*

My phone rang, startling me. I picked it up.
'Please listen to this automated message.
Please say your full name, so we can confirm
You are not being contacted in error.'
A silence then. I thought to end the call,
But the voice, female, bossy, seemed to insist,
I could not disobey... 'John Denzil Trenear.'
Another, longer pause, and then, 'Hello!
Your local Council has brought in a scheme
To help the old and vulnerable in these
Difficult times. It is voluntary and free.
Our carers think it might be helpful to you.
Should you so wish, accredited sex workers
Will visit you and offer sexual
Comfort. It's safe: you have been quarantined
And they have tested clear. These carefully chosen
Young women have lost their livelihood
And so this helps them too: your Council pays.
If you are gay, that too is catered for.
Should you decide to avail yourself of this
Call us on freephone zero five hundred, six thousand,
Any time nine to five in the next two weeks.
All is in strictest confidence. Goodbye.'

My brain was reeling as I dropped the phone
And collapsed into my chair. Was it a hoax?
A trap? I got my specs and an old copy
Of Yellow Pages, staggering under it,
Sat with it in my lap, looked up the Council.
I found that number, listed against Parks
And Recreation. It could be genuine.
Suppose it was, what then? I started shaking.
It was so long since I. I'd surely flop.
I've only once gone with a prostitute;
That was a few years after Jenny's death;
Elsie and I were going through a bad time;
I'd come to London for a conference,
Boring stuff to do with my boring job.
Wandered in Soho, thought to hell with it.
It was anger with Elsie—and God—as much as lust.
The girl was black; I'd wanted that—
To try them. She was at first obliging,
I asked her to put on a suspender belt
And stockings—it was the '70s, they'd vanished—
And she did. When we started it was fine,
But then she wouldn't kiss, which put me off;
It felt so cold and separate that I

Just couldn't come. Impatient, she said
She'd have to finish me with a vibrator.
It worked, but it was like an operation.
In those days hard-ons came so readily,
The flash of a suspender, say, when they
Were still being worn, reminding
Me of my Auntie Peggy, or breasts overflowing
A low-cut dress. Not so, now.
And yet... It would be nice. Or could be.
I feel disturbed, can't face my beans on toast.
'Our carers think...' That's bloody Virginia.
Sorry for me, I guess. So is it part
Of the wider, sinister picture? Aliens?
I feel weak, get myself to bed by nine.
Can't sleep again, tormented by desire
As when I was fifteen, after I'd glimpsed
My Auntie in her corselette and stockings
And she saw that I saw, and smiled,
And did not close the door.

11 *Auntie's bodice*

To break the spell of hopeless sexual longing
I forced myself to turn on the radio
Beside my bed. It's old, the sound was muffled.
Some kind of discussion was taking place
Between a man and woman. I could hear,
Even when leaning close, little of it,
Just the odd phrase. There was a weird
Moment when the woman, who he addressed
Several times as Iris—I couldn't make out
What his name was—said, 'Auntie's bodice'.
That startled me; bodice is so oldfashioned.
It could have been plural, say 'Aunties' bodies',
Referring to Peggy and my other aunt,
Gwen, her companion in their spinsterhood.
But why should they be addressing me?
It made no sense, like everything just now.
Then, in a clearer moment, the man said,
'We'll have to live with the Corona Iris.'
Then again nothing I could hear.
I soon switched off, and lay back down,
Staring up at the darkness, wondering if
I'd misunderstood the offer of Corona.
Perhaps to them it didn't mean the drink,

But something else entirely? Perhaps the name
Of the alien beings who have taken over—
If that's the reason for this madness?
'We'll have to live with'—it or them. He'd sounded
Bleak. I kept on trying to make sense
Of what I'd heard, including Auntie's bodice
Or Aunties' bodies, more and more confused
Until I slept, exhausted.

                             I was woken
By a huge weight on me, making me gasp
And struggle to breathe. Opening my eyes
I saw it was the burka'd woman, Fatima.
Leaning forward, her face, a black mask,
Was inches from mine. Her burka spread wide,
Her thighs engulfed me. I heard a deep voice
Say, 'I have come from the Council, they
Are paying me to service you.' And then,
Much younger and more virile, I was inside her
And she was bearing down on me, pulling back,
Bearing down again, intense and rapt as Jackie
Upon her cello. I could hardly breathe.
I struggled to say, 'I would like to kiss you,'
Fatima.' She shook her head. 'No intimacy,

Just fuck.' That heavy voice and downthrust.
'I am not Fatima. One of her sisters,
Corona Iris. If I had been Fatima,
Aziz, her husband, would have slit the throats
Of both of you.' She gave a booming laugh
And with that, with a heave, I threw her off me,
Jerked up in bed, panting, heart pounding,
Sweat pouring off me, pyjamas drenched,
Already morning light flooding my bedroom.

I can't swear to her exact words, only the sense.
It was, in its way, a lovely, exciting dream,
My first sex since with Elsie, long ago.
My day feels so unreal after it.

12   *Fellow braves*

A day of agitation and distress
Over two phonecalls, both pre-recorded
And fuzzy, the lines bad. The first was from
My surgery advising me about
Something that sounded like 'coping at 90'.
It touched a nerve, I think of it a lot.
I slammed the phone down. I'm not bloody 90!
They know I'm only 84. I hate
The thought of being 90, shrunken and gaga,
Yet I don't want to die before then either.
Fuck Dr Gosling for upsetting me!

Soon after that the bloody Council rang me,
Not, this time, offering a sex worker,
But saying we've all been touched by Corona Iris
And it is frightening, especially for the old
And vulnerable. All have been *touched*!
I guess they couldn't say have had sex with.
So was it real, not just a dream?
Some sort of devilish possession
Like in that horror film—what was it called—
The Exocet? Have I been taken over?
And then they offered, to relieve the isolation,

Eye pads. They gave a number to ring back.

Eye pads! They must believe Corona Iris
Is damaging our eyes, making us blind.
I rushed out to the balcony and gazed down
At the street far below, still strangely empty,
And the few figures who were walking there
Were hazier than they had been yesterday.
The same when, with my specs on, I re-read
Virginia's dismissive letter. Hazier!
The difference might be very slight, but I
Am slowly going blind. Both old and blind,
Unbearable! I gulped for air, half-crazed.
My sight's not bad since I had cataract ops,
Though there's the slowly growing mist
They call immaculate degeneracy.
But this is different—swift. And why eye pads?
It must mean there's disfigurement as well
As blindness. Christ... the gulps for air again.
A dreadful day of blinking, peering at objects,
Testing my sight.

                        But then, in the mid-evening,
I heard again the sound of claps and banging

And rushed out. There they all were, outside,

Saluting me! *Zulu* flashed in, the end-scene.

Tony and I used to love acting that,

Michael Caine as Lieutenant Bromyard

Thinking the Zulus were taunting them

But his Afrikaaner comrade saying, 'No, no!'

With a laugh. 'You couldn't be more wrong,

They're saluting you! saluting fellow braves!'

Now, moved by being applauded yet again,

For a moment I forgot my eyes.

I wished I could say We're all braves at Rorke's Drift,

All battling against bereavement, death,

But could only pump my fists over my head

And shout, unheard of course, 'Thank you! Thank you!'

13 *Awkward moments*

I had to find out what my fate would be
So steeled myself to ring the eye pad number.
A woman answered who spoke in that loud, fluty
Voice that is used for toddlers and old people
As if we're gaga. 'I'm interested in your offer,'
I said. 'Oh good, dear!' 'But I have questions.'
'Of course you would, dear...' They had been attacked
In the *Daily Mail*, she said, which put some off
From ringing, but the progressive Labour Council
Believed—I cut her short: 'Will I go blind?'
There was a long pause, then a chuckle;
'No, my love, no! That's an old wives' tale
Said about masturbation, just to scare.
I'd say you need this service, dear.'
I didn't know what this had to do with eye pads
And found it tasteless; best ignore it, so
Plunged shakily on: 'What kind of disfigurement
Can I expect?' Another silence, then
Her voice was cold: 'That's something you would like?
Well, we do have a girl whose face was scarred
Quite badly by a client—would that appeal?'
She'd lost me totally, the stupid bitch.
She went on, just as coldly: 'We do have one,

Beautiful, but with a prosthetic leg.'
I said, 'What has this got to do with eye pads?'
A pause, and then a shriek of laughter. I had,
She chuckled, the wrong number, this line was
For those in isolation who might need
Sexual comfort.

It left me feeling foolish,
I saw that she was right, I'd muddled up
The numbers. Didn't like the way
She laughed at me, saying, 'No worries darling.'
I made a cup of tea to calm my nerves
Before I tried again. Another fluty
Woman: 'You're calling about the eye pads, dear?'
Yes I said. 'Have you used one before?'
Briefly, I said, after my cataract ops
Three years ago. Just for the first day
While the eye healed. Oh, and as a child
I had some shrapnel in my right eye
From a bomb in the Plymouth blitz.
There was another silence, then she said,
'I think we're at cross purposes,' and explained
The eye pads they were offering were tablets
So we could contact people on the net.

It made me angry. 'Then why call them eye pads?
I don't want one of those'—and rang off.
My anger turned into a huge relief:
I wasn't going blind; at least not quickly.

I went out after dark, to avoid another
Fascist policeman. The streets were empty,
Even the pubs were closed and lightless.
Needing a pee, I found a public toilet
Mercifully open. During the long process
Of leaking urine out, a woman entered,
Quite tarted up, and even in a frock,
So rare these days. Embarrassment stopped me dead.
'Wrong door, madam,' I said over my shoulder.
'It's not,' she snapped; 'I identify as a male.
I've as much right to be in here as you.'
And with that she marched into a cubicle.
I'm not fitted for this world. I've had my time.

14   *Temptations*

For two days I have talked to no one other
Than me in my shaving mirror, scary my wild
White hair. Groceries were left for me outside
Before I roused myself from bed.
Confusing those two phone numbers
Troubles me. My mind has stayed razor-sharp,
Almost as keen as when my primary head
Told mum and dad I was the next Einstein,
And dad, a brilliant but humble carpenter,
Still gaunt from war, still almost a stranger,
Looked proud... But what if now...

I've even thought of flinging myself off
My balcony, but I've always been scared of heights;
Easier than death would be the shame
Of having one of those working girls around,
Doubtless skinny, in leggings, with studs and tattoos,
Enduring her distaste for my decrepit
Form, which she would hide of course but I
Would know it was there. I had my hand
On the phone, ready to lift it, when Elsie
Appeared and snapped, 'Don't be a dolt!
She'd give you some terrible disease.' I said

To her, tears in my eyes, it would only be

For company, not sex. 'Do as you please,'

She said. 'You always did, then lied about it,

As you did about that tart Linda. Telling me

It was just flirty. I knew you bedded her.'

With that she left.

                        It was a shock

To know she guessed, or perhaps found something,

For she was always going through my pockets.

I don't regret it, Linda brought me alive

Again, after I'd been depressed for years

In the wake of Jenny's death—depressed and raging

Against the swine who killed her, poor little mite.

And it was only twice that we made love,

As she was married and we both had

A conscience. Mostly it was just fun, some cuddles,

After laughter and a few drinks in a pub.

I wish I had her picture. She was lovely,

A honey-blonde. And those long shapely legs

In stockings she would wear for me.

Just twice, in our whole marriage, and yet Elsie

Is bitter about it, even though she's dead!

There were never many laughs with Elsie.

Tony found out, his first girlfriend a waitress

At the hotel Linda and I stayed at

Those two times. He confronted me,

There's nothing quite so moral and unforgiving

As a teenage boy. He didn't tell his mother

For her sake, but he turned against me completely.

Just twice, for God's sake! I'd try him with

A phrase from *Zulu*, like 'Why us, Sergeant-Major?'

But he wouldn't come back with 'Because we're here, lad;

Just us, and nobody else,' not after that.

I suppose that film is in my mind so much

As it's the last happy link with my son.

'Now cut along back to your mates, where you belong.'

Linda and I were mates, great mates. I mourn

For those few months of happiness we had,

Wish she were here now, even old. Tears spring.

Where is she now? 'Where are they now,

The old familiar faces?' Where does that come from?

15   *A remote death*

The phone rang, breaking up my day.

'Hi, is that Uncle John?' 'Yes.' 'This is Des.'

Desmond, a Union firebrand, roughly spoken.

'I'm ringing to let you know dad passed away.

Thought you would want to know.' Elsie's brother;

She was never very close to her family

And of course I even less so. 'I'm so sorry.'

'Yeah, well he was old and frail but still it's tough

When a Fascist tosser like Boris can survive

And my dad cops it.' I had no idea

Who Boris was. I said, 'How did it happen?'

'He felt breathless, like a huge weight on his chest

But wouldn't let mum call for an ambulance,

Too scared. Everyone's fucking scared.'

Dread took me over; I'd felt that crushing weight.

'So was it Corona Iris?' 'Hah, I like that!

Good one, mate! Yes, Corona fucking Iris.

Mum couldn't even say goodbye or hold his hand.'

What'—I hesitated—'what's behind it all?'

'If you ask me, mate, it's the fucking Jews,

Fucking Jewish financiers. The stock market

Is rising, when the economy is in the shit.

Where there's profit involved, *cherchez* the Jew.'

'You really think so?' 'Damn right. Hunker down, mate,
They're too powerful to take on. If I say it
Out loud, I'll be drummed out of the Party.
Keep silent and out of sight, mate, like me.
Must go. You okay?' 'Not too bad.' 'Bye then.'

I thought for a while of his father. Dry old stick,
Archie. Stammered. Into the horses. No contact
Since Elsie's funeral. He was no more dead
To me now than he'd been for the past twelve years,
And I felt nothing; but that seemed sadder
Than if I grieved a little, for he was human,
Or had been, and now he was nothing.
Out out, brief candle... Was that Hamlet? I turned
My thoughts to what his son had said
About the Jews. The three or four I've known
Were decent folk; they can't help being clever,
Good with money. And how they paid for it!
I watched with mum and her American friend
While dad was still away that Pathé News
About the relief of Belsen, see clearly still
Those piles of bones being dumped in a great pit
Like thousands of stick insects. I thought Desmond

Was talking shit. But not completely.

Old Miss Pemberthy wildly exaggerated

In calling me the next Einstein, but I've

Analysed, with as keen a mind as any

In London, the weird stuff that's occurred

Right from the first offer of Corona.

Des was wrong to blame the Jews, but right

That this is a conspiracy, and one

So powerful that all we can do is hide.

I'm lucky I was able to heave her off me

In the night before the damage was too great.

She, or is it they, make it seem like sex

And in a dream. It had me fooled for a while.

Poor Archie fell for it, wanted, I don't doubt,

To come. A big mistake. Poor bugger.

And how many thousands of others? Lord knows.

16   *After the dance*

It was clever of Corona Iris

To use sex to attack us, as it's our weak point.

What happened that night has disturbed me

As it was so sudden and unexpected—sex

With a stranger. That's how it had seemed,

And it's brought back a powerful memory

Of RAF Abingdon, when I did my basic training

On National Service. I was 18, had never had

A girl. We'd just had our passing out parade

And we all piled into the battered camp bus,

Me and my mates, to go to a dance in the town.

I didn't dance much there, too shy,

Had a couple of pints, which I wasn't used to,

It was only Corona at home, apart from

Elderberry wine at Christmas. The evening passed,

We all waited for the bus outside in the dark,

Most of us lads smoking. Not me. I could see

Two or three couples smooching, off to one side.

Our bus came, we piled in, it was packed,

The seats along both sides, and the aisle,

All ranks together, the air boozy and gay

In the old, proper sense of the word—not queer.

We moved off with a jolt, the light went out,

And this WAAF officer, standing, was pressed against me

In the pitch-dark. I had seen her in the huddle

Of smoochers, kissing a chap goodnight.

I could smell her heavy wool tunic as she lurched

And swayed, sometimes my face making contact

With it, our old banger bumping along

The pitted road to camp, her feet braced apart.

And I don't know how I had the courage but

No doubt the pints in me helped, but I just

Let my hand hover between her knees

Under the heavy calf-length skirt.

When the bus lurched more strongly my hand

Touched her leg for an instant and

She didn't notice or she didn't mind,

So, God help me, I moved my hand further up

And at the next lurch it touched the bare flesh

Above her stocking, and she still did nothing

Though she must have known by now. I guess

She was feeling randy from drink and the smooching.

So I started feeling her around, flirting with

Her suspenders, so it was really obvious,

And going up higher and then into her knickers

And I heard or felt her gasp, and I was all around

Her fanny and everywhere, up under her girdle
And around the back, spreading her wetness,
My first time ever with a girl. Not just any girl,
An officer! Shit, I could have been court martialed!
None of those next to us, lurching against us,
Had any idea of our silent secret frenzy.
When we reached camp I withdrew my hand
And she moved off slowly with the crowd.
Once in my hut I lay on my pit and smelt
And she was still there. Fragrant and sticky.
And of course I... A WAAF officer's cunt!
Later I would see her cycling around the airfield,
Very poised and snooty. I would salute her.
She didn't have a clue who I was—I guess.

She must be 90 now, if she's alive.
'Coping at 90' as my stupid doctor said.
If she remembers—unlikely—frail, bedbound
In a Home, I hope she is thinking, that night
I felt a stranger's lust for me, a hand
Craving and determined to take its pleasure,
In a young, roaring-drunk crowd in darkness,
And that stirred lust in me, and it was good.

17 *Something romantic*

I was in my armchair, lost to everything,
When I felt my shoulder being gently shaken
And a woman's voice say, 'John! John!
Are you alright?' I opened my eyes and saw
Gazing down at me anxiously my Auntie Peggy,
That was my first thought, then I realised
It was Virginia. 'I'm fine,' I said. She smiled.
I could see her lips as she no longer had
A bandage over her lower face. 'Don't worry,'
She said, 'I'm not contagious as I've had it,
But mildly.' I'd no idea what she meant;
Herpes? 'I saw you slumped aside and mumbling
Rather strangely. I thought you might be ill.'
I told her I often talk to myself, a frailty
Of age. She perched on my sofa, her hands clasped,
And smiled again. 'I hope it was something nice
You talked about?' I was recalling
A romantic moment, I said, as a young man
While serving in the RAF. The image
Of that officer on her bike still hovered, more real
Than Virginia—till she brought out of a bag
Of groceries, triumphantly, a bottle.
I gasped: 'It's Corona!' 'You're right! Lemonade

Not cherryade, I fear.' She said she'd searched
On D-Day—which made no sense, she wasn't born
Till many years after—and a nice Welshman
Who had worked for Corona still had a few,
And sent her this for me. 'He warned the fizz
Would have gone, but it would still be drinkable.'
I thanked her, still confused about D-Day.
But I shan't drink it; Iris is everywhere.

Later, she phoned me, burbling on, bubbly.
She and Emma had been preparing a booklet
Of memories written by old ex-servicemen
In our area, to come out on VE Day.
'How much we owe to our brave servicemen
Such as yourself.' All proceeds from it would go
To veteran charities. They'd quite a few
Nice contributions but could do with more.
'Not about battles but more human interest.
I wondered, John, if you would write for us
That memory in your mind this morning?
It would be wonderful! Our booklet needs
Something romantic, as you said yours was.
Most others are quite dry.' That knocked me back.

'I'm not a writer,' I said. 'No matter, just write it
As it really was.' I thought for a long time;
The people here had clapped me twice; I owed
Them, and our brave veterans, something.
I hadn't fought, had spent my time in the RAF
As a clerk, and in peacetime.
I told her I would try. 'It *was* romantic,
At least it is as I remember it,
But it was also'—I sought the right word—'racy'.
Virginia giggled. 'Racy? All the better,
It will enliven it! I bet you were
A devil in your youth!' 'I'd tone it down.'
'Oh don't, be truthful! There is very little
That's shocking to us today.'

                        And so I'm writing.
The hours go by more quickly. I'm bringing
That lovely young WAAF officer to life.

18   *VE Day*

I wrote, crossed out, wrote and crossed out,
Struggling with words as my dad once struggled,
Planing driftwood. Should I say 'gradually'
Or 'inexorably' my hand slid up her thigh?—
That kind of thing. At long last it was done.
I left it, in an envelope, with my empties
Outside, and while I slept it was collected.
Dreary days followed, but I felt proud
Of what I'd done. There came another evening
When I heard claps and bangings all around
But I felt too embarrassed to go out:
This was too much, too much being praised, applauded.
I even started to wonder, was it for me,
Had they been clapping and banging for someone else?
If so, I had shamed myself by bowing, waving.
But who else could it be? I dismissed the thought
With relief. Then the next morning, when I got up,
I found a package on my mat. A flutter
In my heart as I opened it, and yes
It was the booklet, with a glossy cover
And the title, *Memories of the Brave*. Inside,
A note: 'Thank you so much, John, we love it!
Jinny.' I found my piece, and spent the next

Hour reading it over and over. It looked
Much more impressive, beautifully printed.

It had to be VE Day I thought, and went
Out on my balcony, expecting crowds below,
A street party, but there were hardly any people
Walking around; no cars, just a few cyclists.
It seemed unworthy, disrespectful to
All those who'd given their lives in the great struggle.
My thoughts went back to this day in Penzance
75 years ago. My memories were hazy,
Far hazier than of my WAAF officer,
But I remembered brightness, Union Jacks
And bunting, trestle tables full of goodies,
Sausage rolls, pasties, trifle, saffron buns,
The bustle of women bringing out more
Into the street, loud talk and laughter.
Corona of course, the pop and fizz when they
Were opened. Songs sung like 'We'll Meet Again',
But I recall my aunts, Peggy and Gwen,
Both in their early twenties, bosomy, bright-
Lipsticked, not singing it; or do I just
Assume they didn't, for their fiancés

Had copped it, Gwen's on the beach in Normandy,

Peggy's while on a bombing raid? Perhaps.

At nine years old, one doesn't have much sense

Of other people's grief. I did find mum

Having a quiet cry, back in the house,

And asked her was she wishing dad, a POW,

Was here, and she said yes; but now

I think it's much more likely to have been

Sadness because the American at our party,

Larger than life, a captain in their army,

Who'd been a frequent presence in our house

And often stayed the night, I don't know where,

Would soon be flying home. She'd miss

His generous gifts of Lucky Strikes and nylons

And who knows what else; I would miss

The chewing gum, long coloured strips of it,

Much tastier than our skimpy white ones,

And Hershey bars, and even a German helmet.

Ah yes, it was a day of new beginnings

But also one where loss and death struck home.

19   *Offensive*

Two empty days, then a knock on my door
Cheered me—a person! I saw a young, burly
Policeman standing there. 'Mr John Trenear?'
'Yes.' A copper is always a shock; you think,
They've found me out! He flashed his badge and said,
'I'm DS Sweet, could we have a little chat?'
'Of course.' Ushering him in I offered
To shake his hand, but waving it away—
'Best keep to the two metres. Can we sit?'
We sat down, face to face. 'Can I call you John?'
I nodded. 'John, I won't beat about the bush,
Complaints have been made against you by five women,
Five separate women. They're accusing you
Of a hate crime against them.' 'A hate crime?
I've never heard of that.' He licked his pencil
Then scribbled in his notebook. Looking up:
'A hate crime is a criminal offence
Perceived by the victim or another person
To be motivated by hostility
Or prejudice, based on, in this case, their sex.'
I was so dazed I barely took it in,
But he went on to talk about my piece
In the just-published booklet, where I admitted

To sexual assault by penetration.

'But do I know these women?' 'You don't have to.

They personally feel assaulted, claiming

Your attitude of taking what you wanted

Regardless of that woman's wishes shows

Misogyny. It riled you that a female

Was your superior, so you assaulted her.'

'But I love women!' 'Didn't sound like it!

I'm not arresting you, it's just a chat

At this stage. Of course if the woman herself

Read it and wished to make a complaint you'd be

In even more serious trouble, much more.

A custodial sentence, maximum sentence life.'

I said it was sixty-odd years ago, and he

Responded that there was no limitation.

'I would have stopped immediately if she

Had showed she was unwilling!' 'How could she?

Trapped in the crowd, her feet braced

As the bus veered about! No John, you had her

Just where you wanted her—helpless. But anyway,

She isn't likely to read it, if she's alive,

And though it's a serious crime it's not

As bad as, say, some old Nazi camp guard

At Auschwitz; the CPS would likely

Choose not to prosecute. And you are frail,

And shaking, I can see. Bit of a shock, John.

Look, I'll come back tomorrow, give you time

To think about it and prepare a statement.'

He stood up, fiddled in his pocket, handed me

A card. 'A number for the Samaritans

If you should feel you need it. I don't like

To have to have this kind of conversation

With an old veteran. You take care now, John,

Don't think of doing anything foolish.

He glanced around. 'Where's your computer?...

Lapdog'—lapdog?—'eye pad? smartphone?'

'I don't have any.' 'Ah, you're very wise!

If you'd had one, I'd have had to take it.

I'll see myself out.' He was gone. I sat

Like a zombie in my chair all day, all night.

'I can see how it was, a young lad, but it was wrong!'

The DS wore a smile, but I didn't trust it.

'She couldn't scream, an officer in a male

Dominated service, it would have been shaming;

And the next day she wouldn't know who you were!'

I was trying to hold tears back, but they came oozing.

They had had thirteen more complaints, he said,

Four of them from males on behalf of women.

My voice was husky: 'Virginia—Mrs Rudd—

Said that she loved my piece.' He shook his head.

'She and her fellow editor—her wife

I believe—tell us they found it distasteful,

But felt they couldn't not include it as

They'd asked you for it. Oh, and freedom of speech,

But they acknowledged that is no defence

When persons are offended. They have apologised

And withdrawn all unsold copies. It's a shame,

There were lots of touching, decent memories.'

I wept now openly for a while. He waited.

When I could speak I said, with many pauses,

'It didn't feel at all like an assault.

It felt like—it was an unexpected thrill

We both enjoyed, in our own private world.

It even felt tender'—'Tender!' He gave a chortle.
'Sticking your hand up for a fingerfuck!'
'It wasn't... It didn't seem like... When my hand
First brushed her thigh over her stockingtop
And she didn't flinch away I felt... I felt...
She was alright with this. And when I reached—
You know... well, she was wet, she was aroused,
So how can that be sexual assault?...
In the world I grew up in it was assumed
The man would take the lead, the girl would either
Show it was not on or it was okay.
There was a kind of teasing give and take,
A game both sexes played. Mutual respect.'
Exhausted, I pulled out my handkerchief
And wiped my eyes and blew my nose.
'Things are much different now,' he said; 'more equal.
You can put all that in your statement, John.
But on the point you made, that she was wet,
Aroused—means nothing; that can happen
Even in a rape, it's a purely automatic
Response. Even one of the ladies who've accused you
Admitted, under questioning, she had been
Aroused by it, but that increased disgust

And led to nausea. I think we're done
Here for today. You need a shower, some rest.'

I didn't shower—too tricky at my age—
But had a wash, including 'down around'
As my mum used to order me to do,
Then stretched out on my bed but couldn't sleep.
I wondered were they right? Now I felt shameful,
My whole life seemed disgusting, as I looked back.
I yearned to talk to Elsie, stretched my hand
To touch her folded nightie. She's not come
For far too long. I thought about Sweet's comments.
The present is a foreign country to me,
Like our first holiday abroad, in Spain; we didn't
Understand their language or their ways,
What it meant to be Spanish, not us.
Only we had a passport, could go home.

21 *Good news*

Is it all because of Corona Iris, whatever
It is or they are? Till a few weeks ago
My life was lonely, empty, yet not crazy,
But now... Why did he ask if I have a lapdog?
And these mysterious eye pads, which have nothing
To do with eyes it seems? And DS Sweet,
Who isn't sweet despite his rosy-cheeked
Bland face, he too referred to—I forget her name—
As Virginia's wife. Marriage is the union
Of man and woman as ordained by God.
I can't imagine John Wesley, say, or our own
Great Cornish evangelist Billy Bray
Asking 'Do you take this woman to be
Your lawful wedded wife?' And then, I suppose,
'You may kiss both your brides.' I'm in a madhouse.

In contrast to the applause I was receiving
I'm getting messages through my letter box
Abusing me, telling me I am disgusting,
And some suggesting, in the crudest terms,
What ought to happen to my private parts.
Sweet came again. I hate his baby-face,
He can't be more than 30, 35.

He said he brought good news: it was decided,

In view of my old age and frailty,

Both physical and mental, I'd be spared

The stresses of a trial. I only had

To accept my guilt for a hate crime and

I would be let off with a Caution. 'I'm

Pleased for you, John,' he said with a smug look;

'I fought for that result.' What could I say?

I don't believe what happened on that bus

Was a crime at all; and what does 'hate crime' mean?

You can't look into people's souls to see

Emotions; a crime is just a crime, and thoughts

Aren't punishable. But 'Yes,' I said, 'alright:

I'm guilty.'

        'I'll bring you all the paperwork.'

And then he said, 'It's good you don't have Twitter.'

'Twitter? What's that? I only know birds twitter.'

I didn't understand his explanation,

But he went on to say one of my victims

Had tweeted—tweeted?—extracts of my piece,

The most offensive parts, and this was causing

A 'twitter-storm'. I think that was the phrase.

'So I suggest you stay alert—to quote

The new advice from Boris.' Who is Boris?
'Be careful who you let in. Stay indoors
Completely, as you never know, a tabloid
May have got hold of it and sent
Photographers. I understand, from glancing
At your application for a mortgage, you were
A vicar once?' 'No, briefly in my youth
I was a Methodist lay preacher.' 'A lay preacher!'
He chuckled. 'Meaning you could lay all the girls?'
I ignored his tasteless comment. He continued:
'So, a juicy scandal! The media could
Have fun with that. "Former preacher
Admits to hate-fuelled sexual assault".
They love hypocrisy; like that Ferguson guy
Who ordered us all to stay apart, then had
His married mistress over twice for sex.
Banging away. I admit the slag looks hot.
Take care now.' Gave me a thumbs-up as he left.

I had to get outside, felt claustrophobic.

The streets were busier than they had been

For many weeks, though without traffic jams.

I noticed several people were bandaged up

Around their lower faces. Some strange disease

I have so far escaped. Since almost all

Wore flat shoes, jeans or trousers, loose

Jackets or shirts, the mostly hidden faces

Made it even harder than usual to tell

Women from men. It used to be so easy.

But it was clearly a sharp female voice

Made me look up from my frame. 'Should you

Be out, at your age?' A young white woman

With green hair, her bare arms tattooed with snakes.

She peered at me more closely. 'You're the chap

From up there, aren't you?'—her gaze

Rising to where my flat is—'Who assaulted

That poor girl? You're a vile old man. Wanker!'

Then, with a glare, she marched past me.

I turned and made my slow way back inside.

A ring of the doorbell roused me

After hours of grey torpor. I struggled up,

Went to the door, saw a tall black faceless

Being. Had it been the Angel of Death

I would have welcomed him, but I knew

It was Fatima; beside her, the black-suited,

Black-bearded, smiling Aziz. I let them in.

He shook my hand, and said they had come

Not only with another curry—indicating

Her shopping bag—but also with compassion

For me, and anger at my persecution.

The unexpected kindness made me cry;

He gripped my hand again, and then we sat.

He'd found, he said, I'd been a servant of God.

'We of my faith have great respect for Jesus,

The greatest respect. There is but one God,

One Allah.' I asked would they like some tea;

He shook his head; it was Ramadan, he explained,

And they must fast. 'I just wished to tell you

What you did to that girl was justified.

The Holy Book says man is superior to woman

And she must be obedient and modest;

If she is not she must be beaten. That girl

Tried to raise herself above man in becoming

An officer; then to go dancing and drinking

And riding crammed in with men...
Well, she was just a whore and deserved
The treatment that you gave her. Is that not right,
Fatima?' He addressed her in, I suppose, Arabic,
Explaining. Facelessly she bowed her head.
'So please, my friend, do not scourge yourself.
It would not surprise me if she shaved her pubes
Like almost all white females do today
To increase their shameful pleasure and tempt men,
Not, as with Muslim women, for cleanliness.
Believe me, God honours you for what you did.'
I mumbled, I know not what, and they soon left.

Then the scourge came, I scourged myself
For cowardice. I should have told him what
Idiocy, what foulness, he had spoken.
And ignorance, claiming white girls shave off
Their natural hair, or that this would tempt a man;
Just picturing it made my flesh creep.
I tried to excuse myself: they were my guests,
I didn't wish to upset Fatima,
But knew, in truth, I'd needed his compassion.

23   *Gardens*

Today a nice coincidence. Hating this grim
Tower block, wishing Elsie and I
Had never moved here—but, dear of her,
She needed to be near the Royal Marsden
So she could take part in the cancer trial
And this was all we could afford—
I looked at photos from much happier times.
After my nervous breakdown forced me to
Give up my job in Croydon we went to live
In a small rundown cottage nestling under
The Brecon Beacons. It had a wild garden,
And though I was not much use at first
I made a decent stab at taming it,
But not too much, we liked the stones and nettles,
And doing that, with beauty all around,
Restored me gradually. I even wrote
About its healing power for *Home & Gardens*,
And it was well received. So I was looking
At snaps from that time, re-living them,
When the phone rang. I picked up, dreading
To find it was from the *Sun*, *Express* or *Mail*,
Tabloids that Sweet had warned me of,
But no, it was from the *Garden* newspaper,

A pleasant-voiced, friendly woman. I thanked
The Lord, and after a few seconds I even
Was not surprised, for the Lord works
In mysterious ways. I guessed she'd read
My *Home & Gardens* piece. And so it proved:
She asked me if my views had changed
Since the long-past experience
I'd written about. I told her, 'No,
Although of course I wouldn't have the strength
And energy to do what I did then;
But I like it wild.' 'You like it wild,' she said.
'Yes, wild and rugged. I'm a Cornishman, you see,
A Celt; we don't like it easy or pretty;
Neat cosy beds are not for us; give us
What looks like stony, unyielding ground.'
'Something to overcome?' 'Yes, but of course
I'd take even cosy now, when I am stuck
Alone in a tower block.' 'To clarify,
You liked resistance?' 'Yes.' 'How did your wife
Respond to that?' she asked. 'Oh, Elsie
Agreed with me, and liked to help.' 'She *help*ed you?'
'Often. But mostly she would cook and clean
While I got on with it. Women were different

- 67 -

In those days.' 'Well, I can agree on that!
You've been most helpful. And I must say,
Remarkably honest. Thank you.'

It calmed me. I rested in my chair all afternoon,
Thinking of when I could heave stones, tear out roots,
My mind drifting to *Zulu*, the scene
Where the two Welsh soldiers are on the hill
Watching out for the Zulus, both of them farmers
Back home; and one of them picks up a handful
Of soil and says, 'No goodness in it, man,
Not like back home.'

Elsie had turned up; it was welcome but

She was enraged with me. 'You've lost your mind

Altogether, you old fool! If you ask me,

Your Uncle Harry had more of his mind left

After that German bomb had blown his head off

Than you do!' I winced. That was my mother's story

When I was old enough to be told;

She said I saw his head before the ARP

Chap told me not to look and carried me off.

In later years she blamed my nervous breakdown

On that; but I think it was grief still, locked in,

Over Jenny's death, and willing her killer's death

Despite our Lord's commandment to forgive.

Elsie should have known better not to stir

Everything up, but she was furious and

I really couldn't blame her. I had woken

That morning to find dog poo pushed through

My letter box, along with a newspaper

Cutting, the headline, 'Too shameless to pretend'.

I read the piece and felt sickened. 'Why the fuck'—

I'd never known her swear, brought up like me

By good Christians—'did you tell that woman

You liked sex to be wild and for the girl

To resist you? And worst of all said I
Would often help you do it? Jesus Christ!'
I asked if I could get a word in edgeways
And she fell quiet. I explained how I'd
Been thinking of our Welsh cottage, how
We had been happy there. 'We were, weren't we?'
In a quieter voice: 'Well, yes, we were,
Once you were through the worst of your
Depression.' 'By working on the garden,
Clearing the weeds but leaving the patch of nettles.
So when that woman rang it was easy
To think she was from the *Garden*.' 'You should get
A hearing aid.' 'My hearing's perfectly fine.'

She left. Alone again. I wondered if
Praying would help. I tried to do it but
Did not feel anyone was listening to me.
My faith keeps coming and going, not like
My dad's, though he'd survived the hell
Of Monte Cassino, then a POW,
Then struggled, I believe, with hearing tales
About my mother while he was away.
You could hear real conviction in his fine

Baritone voice, surging through our chapel,

Or singing solos, *If I can help somebody*,

Or in the Negro Spiritual *Deep River*.

Negro wasn't a bad word then. I think

I took to religion partly to please him.

But I was never sure; now even less so.

God comes and goes. He comes and goes.

25   *Holiday tuition*

I look at early photos... Mum and me
And Uncle Harry, a docker, on holiday
With him in Plymouth, I'd guess a year before
The bomb cut our week short. Mum suffered burns
But worse was grief for her brother. She appears
Serious beside my gaunt but smiling dad
Cutting the cake to celebrate his return.
Missing her American captain too, I'd say.

I loved her, but her mood was often sombre
Throughout my teens. That's why I loved escaping
To my Auntie Peggy for a week each summer
In Torquay, where she had a teaching post.
She was always bright, cheerful and giggly,
Hiding her grief, her lost love. Elegantly
Dressed always, even to go to the shops.
I don't understand why she was never snapped up.
There she is on the beach with me, some stranger
Must have taken it for us—lovely and bosomy
In her one-piece bathing suit. I'd be aware of
Her giggly struggle to remove her underwear,
Her frock still on, after she'd unclipped
Her suspenders openly, for anyone to see,

And *I* certainly did. And of course there was
The day I saw her in corselette and stockings
And she merely smiled, struck a pose and said,
'Well, does my new foundation garment slim me?'
Flushed I could only nod, unable to speak.
One day—perhaps the same day—she asked me
Had I been told about sex. I said that dad
Had talked about seeds and holes. She fetched
A big art book and sat beside me with it
Open on our laps. She found a picture where
A naked man and woman lay embraced,
Kissing, and their legs entangled. I
Was spellbound. 'This is how it is,' she said;
It's warm and loving.' She went on turning pages
And showed me a drawing, highly detailed;
It looked like a flower with many petals.
'And this is a woman's genitals, it's called her vulva,
It's where the penis enters and goes deep.
You'll know it one day, John. It's beautiful.'
Three or four times in the week she'd take me
To the pictures. If it was a romantic drama
She would cry softly, if say, an Ealing comedy
We would both laugh and laugh, and if

It was a musical, like 'Oklahoma', we'd both sing
The catchy tunes all the walk back to her flat.
I think she loved me; perhaps I made up for
The child she'd never have. And I—I shed tears—
At fourteen would have loved to marry her.

Virginia came, to apologise, she said,
For what had happened. I couldn't imagine why
I ever thought she resembles Auntie Peggy.
Her smile is harder; I find that with all women
Today compared with those of my youth,
As if they're afraid of smiling at a man.
Over pink trousers—Auntie would have giggled
And said, 'Look at she, you! She's like a clown!'—
She wore a shapeless white shirt inscribed with
Black letters saying her pen is bigger than mine.
A Corona Iris spell? It made me quiver.
Asked what it meant, she said, 'It's just a joke'.
I don't believe her, don't trust her, faced away.
Before leaving she reached into her bag,
Brought out a bottle and handed it to me.
'It's a sanitizer,' she said; 'I think you need one.'
It was outrageous but I decided

Not to be troubled. I'm far saner than her.
She knows it. It's pathetic.

Ah, so it's time again... the claps and banging
Hurled hate at me. The phone's ring was a welcome
Distraction: I picked up. 'Is that my prodigal dad?'
A booming chuckle; confusion; I said nothing.
'It's Tony, dad.' 'Tony!' Shaky, I sat down.
'I read the *Guardian* interview. You old bugger,
Old skirt-chaser! But that Polly is a cruel
Hypocritical bitch, filthy rich, hates
People with second homes, so she's got three!'
He laughed again; I wanted to tell him
I'd never chased skirts, but he spoke more quietly:
'I did admire your honesty. You have balls.
And I learned something. Your taste for violence
Explains what's always puzzled me. I'm into
SM'—I managed to interrupt him, asked him
What that was; got him to spell it, then winced
At his explanation. 'So now I know
I get that from you. Chris said I should ring you
To tell you I sympathised.' 'Who's Chris?'
'My wife, dad!' 'I thought that was Kate.'
'We divorced years ago, you *know* that.'
Feeling foolish, I said I didn't remember
And we've not spoken much. He said it was when

His mum was dying, so I might not

Have taken it in. I agreed I was not quite

In my right mind at that time. 'So you're with Chris.

Tell me about her.' 'Not a her, dad, a he.'

'Your wife is a man?' 'But very feminine,

A lot younger than me. You met him, dad,

He came to the fucking funeral!' 'Did he?'

'You were out of it. I realised I was gay

From about fifteen, but tried to deny it.

The divorce was amicable, Kate and I

Are still friends, and Josh and Anita

Have taken it well, they really like Chris;

Indeed he's wonderful. We're very happy,

Got married as soon as we could, seven years ago.'

There was a silence; I was trembling, felt my heart

Palpitate. He said at last, 'Are you still there?'

I said I needed some water; I'd be back.

I tottered to the kitchen, filled a glass,

Slopping a lot of it, and gulped; went back

To the phone. 'I'm here again, Tony.'

'Chris and I have a daughter, three years old.'

'A child? But how could'—He said it was through

What I thought was a sorrow gate, till he explained.

'Adorable, called Elsie, after mum. She's black.

Chris is Jamaican, so we chose

A black sorrow gate, hoping the child would have

His colour, and she does. It gives him a stake too.

How's things with you? Are you keeping the two metres?'

I was so shaken and confused I was back

In my mind in Croydon, where Tony was born,

And replied, 'No, just a gas meter.'

His booming laugh again. Then he said

To stay safe, and when the lockdown was over

Perhaps they would manage to come down

For a weekend. I said that would be lovely,

Then stupidly quoted *Zulu*, 'Was it like this

For you, the first time?' But he just chuckled

And said, 'Like what? The first time I had

Gay sex? Well, the guy liked it rough, and I

Enjoyed providing it. You'll know how it feels.'

He rang off. I stayed sitting, trembling.

In the world around, all was silent again.

27   *Childe Roland*

'You've only yourself to blame for this,' scolds Elsie.
'For three or four years after I passed away
You received Christmas cards from Kate and Anita,
With affectionate messages.' 'I don't remember—
Did I?' 'You did! And never replied to any,
So they gave up.' I told her I couldn't imagine
I'd be so rude. 'I simply don't remember.'
'You couldn't deal with it—with Tony—reminded
That he was gay. You blanked it all out.
You're very good at that.'

Two days and nights of churning questions
About where life has taken me
To which there were never any answers.
I don't imagine dear old Miss Pemberthy
Thought I would end up here.
I'd won a place at Manchester, or perhaps
It was Birmingham, a good University anyway,
Once I'd finished National Service. I don't
Remember why I changed my plans, decided
To look for a job near home. I became a clerk
At RAF Abingdon; quite liked the quiet life.
And did religion have something to do with it?

A month or two after my brief encounter
With the WAAF officer I and a couple
Of pals who were religious went to London
On a weekend pass to attend a Billy Graham
Revival meeting. There were thousands there
And in the frenzied atmosphere he inspired me.
I think it was my Uncle Harry's head
Also, that there should be more to life than a head
Sprung off more easily than a Corona top.
Did I think Cornwall, deeply Methodist,
Would be the best place to spread the Good News?
Did I long for the salt tang from the Atlantic?
Perhaps both. I really don't know. I found a post
In local government, a desk job. Auntie Peggy
Was disappointed, but I think my parents
Were pleased, as I was the first in my family
To be salaried rather than bringing home
A weekly pay packet. The office was in Camborne,
Working-class, a relic from tin mining.
I don't remember what I had to do.
On Sundays I became a local preacher,
Leading the evening service in scattered hamlets,
Dying as the mines all around had died,

Large, crumbling chapels serving
A handful of old people. My preaching life
Did not last long; I don't recall if I gave it up
Or if I was gently told I was not suited to it.
I had met at a village social Elsie, sweet, buxom
Like Auntie Peggy. We married, Jenny was born,
And when she was five that bloody piss-drunk driver
Mounted the kerb... We had to move away,
We couldn't stay there, Elsie and I agreed.
A vacancy in Croydon... Tony was born,
We got involved in the community
Without ever liking where we were;
Eventually my breakdown and the cottage
In Wales, on sickness pay. Then several years
In Cornwall again, as parents died one by one
And their small, cluttered houses had to be cleared.
Breast cancer struck, the only hope
A trial at the Royal Marsden. She lingered on
For three or four years more.

                    So here I am,
In this grim tower, alone. 'Childe Roland
To the dark tower came.' I used to know that,
Where is it from?... Ah yes, I played the Fool

When we put *Lear* on, badly... None of these paths
I've chosen, thinking clearly. 'Dear God,' I said
To my wildhaired, gaunt reflection,
'You've always been in lockdown, haven't lived.'
I gave myself a ghastly gaptoothed grin,
Thinking of all the sorrow gates.

Curry and cakes

I woke with a feeling of nausea,

Thinking about Tony and his 'wife'.

Back in the Cornwall of my youth

We didn't know homosexuality existed.

I recall a fair, when I was still at school,

At Marazion, looking out at the sea, the Mount.

I was standing between the dodgems and the waltzer;

Amidst the blare a man came sidling up

And asked me would I like a weekend with him

At a hotel. I was silent, he crept away.

I thought, well that was weird, he doesn't know me!

But he was prowling, lusting, wished to thrust...

And now they marry, can raise children

And everyone thinks it's grand...

Another curry was delivered by Aziz,

Who smiled and left at once. He's a kind man.

Then, an hour later, an unexpected caller.

I opened the door to a smiling whitehaired lady,

Who leaned on a walking-stick, breathing

Quite heavily, I guessed in her mid-seventies.

A summery frock, black hose—presentable.

Forgive my intrusion,' she said; 'are you Mr Trenear?

'Yes.' She stuck out her free hand. 'Megan Hughes.'
A Welsh lilt to her bright voice. I like the Welsh,
They're our blood brothers and sisters. 'I think,'
She said, 'we may have met before. Could I
Trouble you for a glass of water? It's a warm day.'
I let her in; she walked steadily and quickly,
Young for her years. 'I've brought you some Welsh cakes,
Baked them myself. Ever tried them?' 'I have,
But not for years.' Water became tea—
She readily accepted my offer. I sampled her
Welsh cakes, and they were good. I found I'd lived
Not far from her native village, Llangorse,
And was racking my brains to see if, through the years,
The decades, I could glimpse the shadow of someone
I'd met, a younger woman—while she was saying
She lived in sheltered housing, not far away,
'Nice enough, but now we're allowed two periods
Of exercise, I'm making the most of it.'
She had been ill, ten days in bed, four days
In hospital—'hence the breathlessness,
But do you know what has saved my life? These!'
She plucked a packet of cigarettes from her bag.
'The fact that I smoke! Would you believe it!

Smoking, they've found, is some guard against it!'

She laughed, and asked to use my balcony.

'Must have a fag.' When she was in again

I heard a trill. She dived into her bag.

It was one of those cordless phones. I hate them.

She listened, said she'd come, then said to me,

'It's an old lady from the Lodge, who's breathless,

Worried she's got it. I think it's only nerves,

But I should go. I used to be a nurse.

I'm really sorry; could I come back tomorrow?'

I said I'd like that. Then she kissed my cheek.

'I'm safe, you see! No need for the two metres.'

She was gone, fast-walking. I touched my cheek.

It may have been the Welsh lilt in her voice
That caused me to seek out some Cornish voices.
I hunted for and put on a recording
Made by a technician pal of my father's
Of my wedding day. The record was dusty, I hadn't
Heard it for decades. We were married in
The Methodist chapel in Elsie's home village,
The slopes around filled with crumbling minestacks
And engine houses that looked like clenched fists
With one forbidding finger raised
As if to say, 'Don't do it!'
I've listened to it rarely because the minister
Who married us said to the congregation
This was a special day, their own dear Elsie
Marrying a young man, deeply respected,
Who had often preached in this very chapel,
'Bringing our Lord Jesus'. It makes me uncomfortable,
For I had less faith than my humble listeners.
But now as I listened again, through the extra crackles
Of the amateurish recording, I could remember
How seriously I vowed, my voice trembling.
I did believe sincerely—at least enough,
But both I and my small congregations knew

I'd not been up to the long spontaneous prayers

Expected of me; I'd try to imitate

The simple local preachers, but it was mostly

Acting—the raised arms and emotional

Fervour, what the Welsh would call *hwyl*...

'O heavenly Father, we pray that you will spare

Our dear Annie Tresidder, suffering so much...'

That kind of thing. So it was painful,

Reminded I'd been an unfit preacher man,

To quote the title of a song I liked

Sung by a woman with a throaty voice

Whose name I have forgotten.

                    What now moved me

Was to hear again, as though it was today,

The lovely, fervent, harmonious singing,

My mum and dad's voices clearly heard

And tugging at my heartstrings... *The voice*

That breathed o'er Eden that earliest wedding day...'

The last hymn, sung while Elsie and I

Were signing the register, was *'Lead, kindly light...'*

The special hymn of the Cornish miners

Wherever they toiled in the world.

How the words must have resonated with them:

'The night is dark, and I am far from home,
Lead Thou me on...' I shed tears hearing it again.
At least they had had each other, the comradeship,
Laughter—which I could hear also
In our Reception at Marks' Cafe in Camborne,
Where roast lamb was served along with Corona,
And through the noise and bustle came Auntie Peggy's
Lilting Cornish accent as she read out messages...
'Here's a telegram from George the Sixth!
Can't be, he've died... Oh no, it's George and Vi!'
With a ringing laugh. I smiled through tears.
'The night is dark, and I am far from home'
Resonated with me too. At the end of the record
I put it back in its sleeve, then into the cupboard,
Sure I would not hear it again. The voices
All dead, the chapel long since become a wine store,
Or is it a meadery? I can't remember.

Another day of un-Londonlike clear skies.

My Welsh visitor came and looked at photos

While I made tea to go with the lemon cake

She'd brought this time, then asked about each one,

Elsie and Jenny, mum and dad, Aunt Peggy

And so on, murmuring sympathy over Jenny,

Seeing my eyes moisten. She said she'd lost

Her son Bryn at thirteen—leukemia.

Her husband Bill had died ten years ago.

After the tea and chat she used my bathroom

And then the balcony for a cigarette.

Returning, said: 'The lockdown's breaking down,

Pollution will soon be back.' This was a chance

To ask her about Corona Iris but

I still wasn't sure I could trust her, so instead

I asked her how and where we'd met before:

'Presumably in the Brecons.' She shook her head:

'It was a long time before you lived there, John.

It was rather strange; when I'd come out of hospital

I tottered down to our communal room.

First time in three weeks. There was no one there

But for old Mrs Bramley, fast asleep;

But I found a copy of *Memories of the Brave*

Someone had left. I glanced through it

And found your piece.' 'Oh my God!' I said.

'I'm embarrassed.' 'No no, it's good, evocative,

And of course stimulating!' She chuckled.

'Age, at least I find, doesn't affect that.

Your piece had a particular impact on me,

As I was at RAF Abingdon in that year,

'55. I've not always been a nurse,

I spent fifteen years in the WAAFs, and was there then.'

'But you couldn't have been,' I exclaimed,

'You weren't old enough!' 'How old do you think I am?'

I understated it tactfully: 'Seventy?'

'Hah! I'm flattered. I'm eighty seven.'

'Good God!' 'Apart from the fags I've tried

To keep in shape, and to stay young in mind.

I remember that old bus, and the dances,

Even snogging after, with a local chap I fancied.

And... I was the only young WAAF officer

To ride around camp on a bike; the others

Were too prissy, afraid they'd show the lads

Their stockingtops as they peddled.' She laughed.

I don't recall the actual incident,

But I'm pretty sure I was the girl you... felt up.'

I buried my head in my hands, groaned, 'I'm so sorry!'

'Don't be!' She leaned forward and stroked my arm.

'You were a young lad, experimenting, exploring.

Another life. Youth is another country.

I could have stopped you if I wanted to,

Believe me! Did that often enough to oafs,

But anyone can see you're a gentle man.

I rang one of the editors

To find out where you lived. A Mrs Rudd.

Didn't tell her why, of course. She made

Me promise I would not abuse you.' She chuckled.

'I need a cigarette,' I said. 'I haven't smoked

For twenty years but I need one now.'

She took my hand and said, 'Come out with me.'

31   *Anger*

She stayed on till quite late, and even made us

Some scrambled eggs, as good as Elsie made them.

Asked if I had wine, but I haven't touched it

Since Elsie couldn't, in her final months—

I didn't want to make her feel deprived.

Megan said I should start again, a glass

Or two of red wine being good for the heart.

I said her visits were doing my heart good

And she promised to come back soon,

And meanwhile we could ring.

                            She rang next day,

And it was warm and nice. We talked about

Our childhood; she too could remember Corona

Now that I mentioned it. I felt I'd made

A friend at last. But when she rang next day

Her tone was very different—angry.

Angry and critical: why did I use

A walking frame? She'd seen me move

Nimbly enough around the flat;

Surely I could manage with two sticks

And visit her, it was only a quarter mile.

'And why, when you love music and have

That huge collection of old LPs

Don't you play them more often? I
Would have loved to hear some of your favourites.
And you don't use the radio or TV.
You say the voices are muffled, but it's because
You're deaf! For fucksake get a hearing aid!'
It was a shock to hear her swear: you don't
Expect elderly ladies to swear. I was angry too
And snapped back at her. How she had no right
To judge me. 'I should know
If I can manage outside on two sticks,
You don't live in my body! As for music,
I do play it sometimes but the stylus
Is worn and I don't know how to get another.'
'Buy something new! A CD player or phone,
Or a lapdog! I couldn't manage without mine;
You can connect with people through it.'
'I don't like dogs.' 'Dogs? No, a computer.'
'I'm no good with machines.' 'But I could teach you.'
Still more arranging my life: 'You said you'd acted
In an amateur company, enjoyed it and
Once or twice played the lead. Here at the Lodge,
We have a play-reading group. The trouble is
We only have two males, and they're both doddery,

Losing their place in the text, then their glasses.
You could join us as a guest.' Then harshly:
'You're younger than you behave, you've lost
Your fucking balls; you had balls on
That bus; you'd better find them again!'

It was upsetting. I felt tears start to prickle
Behind my eyes so said, 'Thanks for the lecture,'
And put the phone down. I felt heartsick,
It was clear she was angry with me still
For what had happened sixty five years ago,
And punished me by softening me up
Then kicking me in what she said I had lost.
Wishing she'd done just that, on the camp bus.
Revenge served cold. A fucking officer
Still. I raged, cried, raged.

32   *Gerontius*

I woke to familiar aching emptiness.

Groceries had been delivered while I slept.

Tediously, pointlessly, I put myself together.

A dull pain, knowing I'd lost my only friend.

I remembered how she'd kissed my cheek,

More tenderness than I'd known for years.

I went out walking—had to escape from gaol.

No one abused me, nor did they smile at me,

They simply didn't notice me,

As in the past; I drew no more attention

Than the drunk or druggie who was propped

Against a wall, head sunken forward.

The crowd flowed by. Unreal city.

Where did that come from? I used to know.

Was it Wordsworth? I ought to read again,

And not just a few pages of Dickens each day.

While I can. Before the fog descends.

I dropped coins into the poor downandout's cap;

He was my other, my brother,

And what need had I of coins?

I rang the number Megan had written down

For me. When I got through I said, 'It's John.

I'd like you to listen to this.' I raised the volume

Of my old radiogram, just at the point

When the Finnish bass Kim Borg was singing,

With his terrible accent but marvellous tone,

'Go forth upon thy journey, Christian soul,

From this world...' It has always thrilled me

And lifted my soul into belief, and always

It brings tears to my eyes. When it was over

I dimmed the volume, returned to the phone, and said,

'Could you hear it?' 'Yes, it was powerful,

What was it? I've never heard it before.'

'It's from Elgar's *Dream of Gerontius,*

About an old man dying. I first heard it

As a teenager in Penzance, performed in church.

All locals—my dad sang that. It was one of

The first works I bought in my twenties, two LPs.

I've only played it twice before in thirty years,

Once after my dad died, then after Elsie.

It moves me too much, Megan—I always cry!'

'Tears can be good,' she said. 'I'm glad you've played it.

And I'm glad you called me; I was going

To call you later. I want to apologise

For yesterday. I was in an angry mood,

Not anger at you but at—oh, leukemia... God!
It was Bryn's birthday yesterday.'
'Oh my dear,' I said, 'I understand.' 'Of course!
We began in war and shall end in plague,
But far worse are our losses in between.
He would have been sixty. It was a bad day.
A bad hair day.' She chuckled. More lightly then:
'My hair's a mess, it needs a trim.' I said,
'What about mine—it's a Yukon wilderness.'
'Oh, your white mane suits you,' she said. 'I like it.'
Then she went back to her son, in plangent tones,
Saying she had not only lost a son
But grandchildren, probably. That I had a new one,
A new Elsie. 'A black Elsie!' I said. 'Does that
Bother you?' 'Oh no, the colour's no problem.
There's nothing quite like a black gospel choir.
I wouldn't have liked the mother to be German.'
'You ought to... No, I mustn't be bossy again.'
With her Welsh lilt: 'I'll come tomorrow, is it?'

That old-time religion

I was again a preacher man, praying loudly

In Elsie's home chapel at Treskillard. She

Was in a front pew, mostly old people behind her.

But it was also earlier; we had lost the war

And were now strangers in our own land

Under the jackboot. I was praying

In the fervent tones of the genuine local preachers,

Swaying about in the pulpit. I remembered,

When I woke, snatches of it... 'We pray, dear Lord,

The day will come when Churchill

And our brave forces will sweep across the sea

From Canada, in a mighty host, to overwhelm

Satan and all his demons. In the meantime,

We pray you will teach us to abide in patience,

To carry this Cross, which is nothin' at all like

The heavy Cross your only-begotten Son

Had to bear, the dear of 'im.' After that

It's a jumble, about the Gestapo and Hitler Youth,

Casting stones at us for thinking the wrong thoughts,

'As they done to poor crippled-up Willie Cox,

My wife's grandfather...'—he had been wounded

In the First World War. And how 'these heathens'

Had lost all sense of sin. 'Sin has vanished

Like Camp coffee...' Camp coffee! I had forgotten
That nasty stuff. When I had finished the prayer
'In the name of the Father, Son and Holy Spirit'
Auntie Peggy ghosted up to me—the first time
I can remember seeing her in a dream.
She hugged me and said I'd been very brave
To speak out like that, which gave me a warm glow.
She was very clear, in a smart blue outfit,
A pillbox hat and white gloves. She said, smiling,
She was wearing the corselette I liked
And put my hand on her plump stomach
So I could feel its tightness. Still with a smile:
'You should have been as brave in Torquay;
The door was open.'
                                    I lay after,
Deeply moved by her appearance to me;
Also a little churned up by her last remark;
I have sometimes wondered if...
I made an effort to remember the vivid dream
So that I could tell it to Megan.
I related it, omitting the last part from
Embarrassment, when she came in the late afternoon.
'Camp coffee!' She chuckled. 'I'd forgotten it,

Mercifully!'

She winced, biting on a piece of the delicious
Steak she had fried. 'I've lost a filling,' she said;
'Of course all the dental surgeries are shut.'
'Is that because of Corona Iris?' She cocked her head,
Puzzled. 'Corona Iris?' 'Yes. Whoever she is,
Or they are, causing havoc. Do *you* know?'
She chuckled. 'It's Corona virus, John;
A virus. With a V, as in Vera Lynn's vagina!'
Revelation came: 'Aaaaah!' then I laughed,
Echoing her; my first laugh for many years,
And a huge weight lifting. 'I'll try a hearing aid.'
She stood up. 'Poor dear! I want to give you a hug.'
We hugged, and that felt good too. I heard her sigh,
Then she said, 'I don't have many hugs these days.'

While we were eating and taking sips of wine—
She had brought two miniature bottles of Merlot—
We had on in the background a Welsh choir
Which she had conjured miraculously
From her tiny phone. I knew most of the pieces,
And in the quieter ones, like the tender *Myfanwy*,
We joined in with ageing but passable voices,
I humming as I didn't know the words,

But most importantly we harmonised.

'Only the Welsh and Cornish can do that,'

I said. My humming ended abruptly when

A coughing fit came on. I couldn't stop it.

She rushed to bring me water. At last I caught

My breath and gasped, 'I've got the virus, Megan!'

She asked who I'd been close to in the past ten days

Apart from herself. I told her an Asian neighbour

Bringing me curry, just before she'd come

For the first time. 'For a few seconds only.'

'Too recent,' she said. 'And too brief. It's very

Very unlikely. You're not used to singing

Or wine, that probably did it.' She patted my hand.

'But that was a shock; I need a cigarette.'

As she was heading for the balcony

Without her stick, slightly stooped, her large bum

Tightening an ankle-length, ageing skirt,

I saw for the first time her actual age;

I felt, strangely, a pang of tenderness,

Realised I'd thought only of myself and the dead.

I decided not to worry about the cough

Though it had frightened me. She'd been a nurse.

When she returned she seemed lost in her thoughts,
Bowed over her glass, which she was sliding
Around; her bosom, drooping but comely,
Almost touching it. At length, rising, she said
Quietly, 'This is probably too soon... You've not seen
The Lodge yet and my flat. It's pleasant,
The building, not too big, it's human. It has
A pleasant garden. This tower block is bleak.
I just wondered—if you like it when you see it—
You might consider sharing it with me?
As friends. I've two bedrooms. I've outlived
My friends, and really miss the company of men.
Is it something you might consider?
I know it's a big decision.' I was dumbfounded.
Stirred, excited even, but also panicky—
How would Elsie find me? 'I'm very touched.
Yes, I would consider it. But why me?' Her face
Softened, looked shy and young. 'One reason, John,
Is that you're the one man still alive who once
Desired me. As a woman. However briefly... Also
I think you'd stopped living, but are promising!...
Well, and life is too uncertain to be cautious.'

'We're clapping for the carers, cariad.'

'Aaah...' We stayed outside, the evening mild.

'I did tell you one white lie,' she said, linking

Her arm with mine. 'I thought, the truth can wait.

Of course I remember! Girls can get

Horny too, and I was no delicate

Snowflake. I thought, whoever he is,

His touch feels nice, respecting an officer

In being softly-softly—and he's got balls!'

Time passed, in which I only felt the touch

Of her arm. Then I said, 'Wasn't Iris the rainbow

Goddess?' 'It sounds right.' 'I like her;

She comes at her own will not ours. Back home

We never knew when the Corona lorry

Would come. I'd think it must have passed us by.'

Further Titles

Hunters in the Snow
By D.M. Thomas

Vienna in the early 20th century was, in the words of our protagonist and narrator, a soulless, syphilitic whore of a city; a turbulent and bubbling melting pot of races, creeds and politics, rapidly expanding as it strained to contain the ever-increasing multitudes. In such places the nightmare moments of modern history are conceived. This novel is a fictionalised account of those who were to change the very collective psyche of mankind. It is a vivid and poignant portrayal of the sometimes thin dividing line between becoming good or evil.

D. M. Thomas is a British novelist and poet, born and living in Cornwall. His novel *The White Hotel* was an international bestseller and shortlisted for the Booker Prize. It is rightly considered a modern classic, translated into more than 30 languages. John Updike said of the book: 'Astonishing ... A forthright sensuality mixed with a fine historical feeling for the nightmare moments in modern history, a dreamlike fluidity and quickness'; the statement could equally be applied to *Hunters in the Snow*.

Paperback, 164 pages. ISBN 978 1 908878 19 9. Also available on Kindle.

All Cornwall Thunders at My Door: A Biography of Charles Causley
By Laurence Green

All Cornwall Thunders at My Door is the first full biography of Charles Causley to be published, originally published to coincide with the 10th anniversary of his death in 2003. Laurence Green has compiled a great deal of information concerning Causley's life in Cornwall and beyond, of his personal history, his influences and motivations, helping to give context to the great legacy left to us by "the greatest poet laureate we never had."

"This is the first biography of Charles Causley, and takes us towards the heart of a marvellous poet and deeply intriguing man. It's all well done: clear, sympathetic, appreciative and shrewd. Everyone who loves Causley's poems will want to read it." — *Sir Andrew Motion*

"...it has been meticulously researched using archive material and the personal reminiscences of people in Launceston and elsewhere who knew Causley. Covering his early life, wartime service, teaching career and the years of success, Green provides not only a truthful overview of this literary giant but does so in the most entertaining of styles." — *Simon Parker, The Western Morning News*

Includes photographs not previously published and a foreword by Dr Alan M. Kent.
Paperback, 220 pages. ISBN 978 1 908878 08 3. Also available on Kindle.

The Last Waltz: Poems
By D.M. Thomas

In both his poetry and his novels, such as the iconic world-bestseller *The White Hotel*, D.M. Thomas has followed his own vision, ignoring the fashionable and the expected. The Last Waltz is no exception. The impression it leaves is of experience, personal and historical, distilled over a life stretching from the threat of Hitler to the threat to freedom of thought and speech today. The moods vary, from grief to controlled anger to satirical humour; the themes, from falling in love on his first day at Infants school to a royal wedding competing in our news (successfully) with Palestinians being massacred. All explored with immense assurance in a rich variety of forms.

"There aren't many poets in England as good as Thomas." — *The Guardian*.

D.M. Thomas is an internationally known poet and novelist. His third novel, *The White Hotel*, considered a modern classic, has been translated into more than thirty languages. He lives in his native Cornwall with his fourth wife Angela.

Paperback, 94 pages. ISBN 978 1 908878 22 9.

A Complete History of Cornwall
By Thomas Cox

Transcribed from an original copy, published in 1720 by Thomas Cox as part of *Magna Britannia et Hibernia, Antiqua & Nova*, this new edition of Cox's rare partwork *A Compleat History of Cornwal* is a faithful reproduction of the original and contains a topographical description of Cornwall, as well as accounts of the Earls and Dukes of Cornwall and other worthies, the Natural History, an Ecclesiastical History and learned divines, an account of the parliamentary boroughs and corporations and a comprehensive gazetteer. This new edition, produced to commemorate the 300th anniversary of the original, also features all of the original illustrations, including Robert Morden's contemporary map of Cornwall, and has an Introduction by Chris Bond.

Paperback, 156 pages. ISBN 978 1 908878 15 6.

A Child of Love and War: Verse Memoir
By D.M. Thomas

D.M. Thomas, author of the iconic world-bestseller novel *The White Hotel*, explores here some of the key emotional and sexual events and relationships in what has often been a turbulent inner and domestic life. The result is a brilliant, searingly honest and moving verse memoir. The period covered is from his birth in 1935 to the death of his second wife in 1998. He is the winner of a Cholmondeley Award for his poetry.

"There aren't many poets in England as good as Thomas." — *The Guardian.*

D.M. Thomas is an internationally known poet and novelist. His third novel, *The White Hotel*, considered a modern classic, has been translated into more than thirty languages. Three more of his most recent works, *Hunters in the Snow* (2014), *Corona Man* (2020) and *The Last Waltz* (2021) are also published by the Cornovia Press. He lives in his native Cornwall with his fourth wife Angela.

Paperback, 280 pages. ISBN 978 1 908878 23 6.

Following 'An Gof': Leonard Truran, Cornish Activist and Publisher
By Derek R. Williams

Len Truran was, until his death in 1997, a highly influential figure within the fields of politics and culture in Cornwall. He joined Mebyon Kernow in 1964 and, over the years, acted as both secretary and chairman of the party. His publications, under the imprint of Dyllansow Truran, are widely recognised as being seminal in the story of Cornish publishing.

In this book Derek R. Williams explores the life of Len Truran, from his childhood through to his pivotal role in Mebyon Kernow and the campaign for the creation of a Cornish Assembly and on to the remarkably prolific and influential publisher he became.

"Derek Williams is to be congratulated for his handling of a most diverse and complex subject ... Leonard Truran was a dynamic force, active from the 1960s onwards in raising the sense of pride in Kernow through diverse means ... Derek Williams's well organised, highly readable book will preserve his memory for generations to come." — *Donald Rawe, The Cornish Banner.*

Paperback, 104 pages. ISBN 978 1 908878 14 4.

Gathering the Fragments: The Selected Essays of a Groundbreaking Historian
By Charles Thomas

This selection of work by the late Professor Charles Thomas, Cornwall's leading historian at the time of publication, focuses on the more elusive titles from his long and illustrious career and covers the whole range of his output from folklore and archaeology to military and local history, and from cerealogy to cryptozoology. The book also includes unpublished material, as well as specially composed introductions to each chapter, a full biography and a select bibliography.

Chapters featured include: A Plea for Neutrality (*New Cornwall*, 1955); Youthful Ventures Into the Realm of Folk Studies - Present-day Charmers in Cornwall (*Folk-Lore*, 1953), Underground Tunnels at Island Mahee, County Down (*Ulster Folklife*, 1957), Archaeology and Folk-life Studies (*Gwerin*, 1960); What Did They Do When it Rained in 1857? (*The Scillonian*, 1986); Home Thoughts from Abroad (*Camborne Wesley Journal*, 1948); The Day That Never Came (*The Cornish Review*, 1968); *Camborne Festival Magazine* - The Camborne Printing and Stationery Company (1971), The Camborne Students' Association (1974), Camborne's War Record, 1914-1919 (1976), The Camborne Volunteer Training Corps in World War One (1983), Carwynnen Quoit (1985); Jottings from Gwithian (*The Godrevy Light*) - How Far Back Can We Go? (2006), Ladies of Gwithian (2007); Two Funeral Orations (unpublished) - Charles Woolf (1984), Rudolf Glossop (1993); Archaeology and the Mind (unpublished) (1968 inaugural lecture, University of Leicester); The Archaeologist in Fiction (1976); Archaeology, and the Concept of Cornishness (unpublished) (1995 memorial lecture, Cornwall Archaeological Society); A Couple of Reviews - Lost Innocence: Archaeologists as People (*Encounter*, 1981), The Cairo Trilogy (*Literary Review*, 2001); An Impromptu Ode - To A.L. Rowse (1997); *The Cerealogist* - An Archaeologist's View (1991), Magnetic Anomalies (1991/92); Two Cryptozoological Papers - The "Monster" Episode in Adomnan's Life of St. Columba (*Cryptozoology*, 1988), A Black Cat Among the Pictish Beasts? (*Pictish Arts Society Journal*, 1994).

Professor Charles Thomas CBE DL DLitt FBA FSA was a former President of the Council for British Archaeology, the Society for Medieval Archaeology, the Royal Institution of Cornwall, the Cornwall Archaeological Society, the Cornish Methodist Historical Society and The John Harris Society.

"Most of us know of Charles Thomas through his major contributions to our knowledge of the early medieval period. But none of this work, save for two important contributions on cryptozoology, appears in this book. Instead we are treated to a range of material, both published and unpublished, on other matters that have attracted his interest. Cornwall, unsurprisingly, is a major theme but without anything from the journal *Cornish Archaeology*. Here the pieces are from publications such as *The Scillonian, Camborne Festival Magazine* and *The Godrevy Light*. And the range is as eclectic as the sources. Local and military history, folklife, biography, a review of fiction, crop circles, even his previously unpublished inaugural lecture as professor of archaeology at Leicester, all make an appearance. The book concludes with biographical details and a select bibliography. There is much here that you will not have read before, and it's full of wonderful and unexpected revelations." — *David Clarke, British Archaeology 127.*

"Subtitled The Selected Essays Of A Groundbreaking Historian, it not only pays tribute to the breadth of Cornwall's leading historian's scholarship but is also an anthology in which every one of its two dozen or more pieces burns with the author's love for his native land and emphasises the fact that if anyone deserves to be now wearing the mantle of the late A L Rowse as our "greatest living Cornishman", then it has to be Professor Charles Thomas. As engaging as it is erudite and as rich, this is a book which should be on the menu of any reader with an interest in Cornwall and all things Cornish." — *Frank Ruhrmund, Western Morning News.*

Edited by Chris Bond. Paperback, 216 pages. ISBN 978 1 908878 03 8.

Cornwall's Historical Wars
By Rod Lyon

Rod Lyon, BBC Radio Cornwall presenter and former Grand Bard of the Gorsedh Kernow, takes the reader on a fascinating journey through the ages, and through the forgotten wars between the Cornish and their old enemies, the English, revealing a history not taught in schools, and one missing from the 'official' history books. From the early wars with the Saxons, through the rebellions of 1497 and 1549, and on to the Civil War, Rod traces the bloody events which helped to shape the culture and national identity of the Cornish people. This book is essential reading for all those who want to learn the truth about Cornwall's hidden history.

Paperback, 112 pages. ISBN 978 1 908878 05 2.

Cornwall
By Thomas Moule

Thomas Moule's topographical account of Cornwall is taken from the 1838 edition of The English Counties Delineated and is full of detail concerning the seats of the gentry, the monuments in the churches, the history of the parishes and boroughs and the numbers of houses and inhabitants. This fully-indexed edition is a useful source of information for local historians and for those interested in the Cornwall of 170 years ago. The cover of the book features part of Thomas Moule's map of Cornwall taken from the original edition.

Paperback, 186 pages. ISBN 978 0 9522064 6 0. Also available on Kindle.

The Fifties Mystique
By Jessica Mann

Many young women 'long to put the clock back to the post-war years when life seemed prettier and nicer.' In this book Jessica Mann demolishes such preconceptions about their mothers' or grandmothers' young days, showing that in reality life was uglier and nastier.

Born just before WW2, she grew up in the post-war era of austerity, restrictions and hypocrisy, before anyone even dreamed of Women's Lib. The Fifties Mystique is both a personal memoir and a polemic. In explaining the lives of pre-feminists to the post-feminists of today, Mann discusses the period's very different attitudes to sex, childbirth, motherhood and work, describes how she and other young women lived in that distant world with its forgotten restrictions and warns against taking hard-won rights for granted.

Jessica Mann was the author of 22 crime novels and 4 non-fiction books. As a journalist she had written for national newspapers, weeklies and glossy magazines and was the crime fiction critic of *The Literary Review*.

"Jessica Mann analyses the decade with forensic precision – stripping away the rose-coloured specs for good" — ***The Daily Mail***

"thoughtful and emphatic ... a richly readable and persuasive piece of work" — ***Penelope Lively, The Spectator***

an "excellently readable book" — ***Katharine Whitehorn***

"Her battle cry is full of vivid descriptions of the grim, snobbery and casual misogyny of postwar Britain. A crime-writer by trade, her barely veiled exasperation only makes the polemic more enjoyable ... " — ***The Mail on Sunday***

"an extremely engaging read: revealing, touching, informative and occasionally comic." — ***Simon Parker, The Western Morning News***

"She recalls the grime of the 50s: endless stinking nappy buckets; smog; inadequate washing facilities; body odour whenever people were crowded together. She recalls boredom and isolation, and suspects both the child-rearing experts and the government of a concerted push to get mothers back home after the war, so that there would be jobs for the returning 'boys'. And she recalls the unacceptability of talking, or sometimes even knowing, about sex, female anatomy, and cancer. She is bang on" — ***Baroness Neuberger, The Jewish Chronicle***

First published by Quartet Books in 2012.
Paperback, 224 pages. ISBN 978 1 908878 07 6.

The Wheal Margaret Adventure: A Calendar of Agents' Reports and Associated Records, 1857 to 1875
By Chris Bond

A calendar of Agents' Reports, Correspondence and Mine Reports relating to Wheal Margaret Mine in the parish of Lelant in West Cornwall. The records transcribed here date from 1857, shortly after the mine was re-opened, up to 1875, shortly after the decision was made to quit the adventure. They give a detailed account of the workings of each lode in the mine; the promise and the problems; the fortunes and the failings. Any comprehensive series of reports such as this provides a valuable historical background to the story of tin mining in Victorian Cornwall. Edited and with an introduction by Chris Bond, who previously edited the catalogue of the Boulton & Watt papers held at the Cornwall Record Office, and who additionally transcribed a substantial part of the same.

Paperback, 130 pages. ISBN 978 1 908878 15 1.

Dowsing
By Thomas Fiddick

This reprint of a rare and obscure pamphlet, originally published by Thomas Fiddick of Camborne in 1913, details the various experiments which he undertook whilst dowsing for mineral lodes in his native Cornwall, as well as giving a potted history of mineralogical dowsing in the area. It also gives details of his "Dowsing Cone" and instructions for its use. This book is an invaluable resource for those who study or practise the art of rhabdomancy, or for those who wish to learn more concerning the history of mining in Cornwall. Edited and with an introduction by Chris Bond.

"Great stuff! ... fascinating." — *Professor Charles Thomas.*

Paperback, 44 pages. ISBN 978 0 9522064 8 4.

Dead Woman Walking
By Jessica Mann

Gillian Butler moved away from Edinburgh 50 years ago, or so her friends thought. When her murdered body is found, they must try to remember who last saw her alive. Perhaps it was Isabel, now a novelist and people-tracer, or the twice widowed Hannah, or the psychiatrist, Dr Fidelis Berlin, an expert on child abuse, abandonment, abduction and adoption, who had herself been an unidentified infant rescued from Nazi Germany and now hopes to discover her real name at last. Fidelis Berlin and other characters from Mann's earlier books reappear in this tense, gripping tale of vengeance, family ties and the mystery of identity.

Jessica Mann was the author of 22 crime novels and 4 non-fiction books. As a journalist she had written for national newspapers, weeklies and glossy magazines. She was the crime fiction critic of *The Literary Review*. Jessica and her late husband, the archaeologist Professor Charles Thomas, lived in Cornwall.

"This is a complex and chilling story, with many shifts of perspective and timeframe. The quality of the writing shines out. The question of changing identity is crucial — not just of individuals but of women in British society over the last half-century. Beneath it all is an elegiac note of regret, a sense of wrong choices with long consequences." — *Andrew Taylor, The Spectator*

"As ever with this author, the intelligent (and complex) texture of the novel matches its sheer storytelling nous." — *Barry Forshaw, crimetime.co.uk*

"Engaging, enthralling and hugely entertaining." — *Frank Ruhrmund, Western Morning News*

"There is a very striking climax, but this is also a novel of ideas, about feminism, family and literature … As you would expect with Jessica Mann, it's a very well-written as well as a poignant book, and I'm delighted to have read it." — *Martin Edwards, Do You Write Under Your Own Name?*

Paperback, 192 pages. ISBN 978 1 908878 06 9.

Godmanstone Blues
By Chris Bond and Andy Paciorek

Defy not the urge to buy! For this book could save your very living soul.

Poetry and prose by Chris Bond, with original illustrations by the acclaimed artist Andy Paciorek.

Paperback, 100 pages. ISBN 978 1 908878 17 5. Also available on Kindle.

Chinese Whispers
By Andrew Birtles

Dear Reader, you probably know the party game "Chinese Whispers" but if you don't here's what happens. A group of your friends and family get together, someone starts off with a sentence, in this case "Piglets in pyjamas danced on tiptoes round a tree". Then they whisper to the next person who whispers what they heard to the next and so on and so on...

You'll find it changes every time because people don't hear properly what's been said. Oh, and by the way, you'll be the last person to hear the message so listen very carefully while you're reading this book because without you there won't be a final page.

Yours sincerely, Andrew Birtles

P.S. You may be unfamiliar with some of the words used, so brief descriptions have been included to enhance your enjoyment.

Paperback, full colour, 52 pages. ISBN 978 1 908878 09 0. Also available on Kindle.

Shut away!: My early days fishing out of Newquay

By Rod Lyon

Rod Lyon, former Grand Bard of the Gorsedh Kernow, recollects his early days fishing out of Newquay, "in the days before modern electronic aids, man-made fibre ropes, twines and cords, plastic 'skins' and floats instead of cork ... when navigation to and from the gear was by dead reckoning, using only a watch and a compass, with only experience telling you what to allow for with the tide." Rod illustrates, in both words and pictures, the techniques and the equipment used in those bygone days, and along the way remembers some of the more notable characters, both Cornish and Breton, who frequented 'down Quay'. The book also includes a gazetteer of his favourite fishing grounds.

Paperback, 120 pages. ISBN 978 1 908878 01 4.

Antiquarian Notes on the Prehistory of Cornwall
Edited by Chris Bond

This is the first volume in a series dedicated to reproducing some of the long-forgotten articles from historical journals relating to Cornwall's illustrious and ancient past. The articles themselves are taken from a variety of publications, both local and national, and from a wide span of time. To have these valuable sources in a set of compact volumes makes not only for an interesting read but also a useful tool for reference. This initial volume includes: Account of Antiquities discovered in Cornwall, by the Rev. Malachy Hitchins (*Archæologia* 15, 1806); Pendarvis Quoit, Cornwall by J. S. Storer and J. Greig (*Antiquarian and Topographical Cabinet*, 1808); The Hurlers (*Light From the West*, 1833); Some Account of the Opening of a Barrow near Newquay by The Rev. Canon Rogers (*Report of the Royal Institution of Cornwall*, 1840); King Arthur's Hall by S. R. Pattison (*Report of the Royal Institution of Cornwall*, 1852); The Celtic and Other Antiquities of the Land's End District of Cornwall by Richard Edmonds (*Archæologia Cambrensis*, 1857-8); Notes on Stone Circles by J. T. Blight (*The Gentleman's Magazine*, 1868); Remarks on the Stone-Circles at Boscawen-un and Boskednan in West Cornwall by E. H. W. Dunkin (*The Reliquary Quarterly, Archælogical Journal and Review*, 1869-70); Cornish Antiquities Viewed in the Light of Modern Research by William C. Borlase (*Transactions of the Penzance Natural History and Antiquarian Society*, 1880-81); Duloe Stone Circle by C. W. Dymond (*Journal of the British Archaeological Association*, 1882); Prehistoric Remains in Cornwall: 1 - East Cornwall by A. L. Lewis (*Journal of the Anthropological Institute of Great Britain and Ireland*, 1896) and Note on an Unrecorded Cromlech in North Cornwall by Henry Dewey (*Journal of the Royal Institution of Cornwall*, 1911). The volume also contains a bibliography and an introduction by Chris Bond.

Paperback, 160 pages. ISBN 978 1 908878 21 2.

For further details see cornovia-press.wikidot.com

www.ingramcontent.com/pod-product-compliance
Lightning Source LLC
Chambersburg PA
CBHW071323130626
46556CB00004B/1725